AND THEN HE Kissed Me

AND THEN HE
Kissed
Me
STORIES of Love,
Heartbreak
& OTHER Unnatural Disasters

Katie Dale ♥ Cathy Kelly

Abby McDonald ♥ Monica McInerney

Sinéad Moriarty ♥ Joanna Nadin

Adele Parks ♥ Madhvi Ramani

Dyan Sheldon ♥ Sarah Webb

WALKER
BOOKS

This collection first published 2013 by Walker Books Ltd
87 Vauxhall Walk, London, SE11 5HJ

2 4 6 8 10 9 7 5 3 1

Anthology © 2013 Walker Books Ltd
"Star-Crossed" © 2013 Katie Dale
"Supercool" © 2013 Cathy Kelly
"Extracurriculars" © 2013 Abby McDonald
"My Embarrassing Mother" © 2013 Monica McInerney
"Lost in Translation" © 2013 Sinéad Moriarty
"The Movie Kiss" © 2013 Joanna Nadin
"All of a Sudden" © 2013 Adele Parks
"Dog Days" © 2013 Madhvi Ramani
"Just a Friend" © 2013 Dyan Sheldon
"My First Kiss" © 2013 Sarah Webb

Cover photograph © Jean Luc Morales / Getty Images
Typograpy © 2013 Walker Books Ltd
Chalk Effect Typography by Joel Holland

The moral rights of the contributors have been asserted

This book has been typeset in Sabon

Printed and bound in Great Britain by Clays Ltd, St Ives plc

British Library Cataloguing in Publication Data:
a catalogue record for this book is available from the British Library

ISBN 978-1-4063-4003-7

www.walker.co.uk

"Love is not love
Which alters when it alteration finds,
Or bends with the remover to remove:
O no! it is an ever-fixed mark
That looks on tempests and is never shaken"
– William Shakespeare, *Sonnet 116*

What better way to open a romance anthology than with the immortal words of Shakespeare? The stories in this collection are sometimes tender, sometimes funny and sometimes sad – but all are a celebration of love, however fleeting. We hope you enjoy reading them as much as we enjoyed writing them!

STAR-CROSSED

Katie Dale

"Roses are red, violets are blue...

What should come next? I've no bloody clue."

I screw up the page in my fist. I can't believe it's the last week of the summer holidays, and I'm sat on a beach *still* writing this crappy love poem for homework.

"Write from the soul," Mr Gibbs had said. "I don't want hearts and flowers; I want the exquisite torture of falling hopelessly in love."

Simple, eh? I glare at the heap of crumpled rejects. Everything I write sounds hollow, tacky – like a supermarket valentine's card. *This* is exquisite torture – a sixteen-year-old lad trying to write a bloody love poem! Like love even exists.

Don't get me wrong – I've had girlfriends. A few, anyway. Well, OK, I've had a few snogs with Jenny Pritchard behind Tesco's, but, well, let's just say it wasn't my *heart* she set throbbing, and I'm not going to write a poem about *that*.

I toss my notebook aside, totally uninspired. And if there's anywhere on earth I should be inspired, it's here: the perfect beach on the perfect Greek island, the perfect breeze rippling across the perfect waves – and sending my papers scattering. Shit. I scrabble after the poems, lunging and diving as they scuttle across the beach.

"G'day."

I turn.

And there she is. The girl of my dreams. Tall and tanned, her curly dark hair tumbling wildly around her shoulders as she smiles down at me with eyes the colour of melted chocolate.

"Hi." I gulp.

"Is this yours?" She holds up a crumpled piece of paper.

Oh God.

What is love? It's just a hoax.

One of life's most brutal jokes.

Kill me now.

"Are you a poet?"

"Hardly. It's coursework. We have to write a love poem. It's stupid."

She raises an eyebrow. "Poetry? Or love?"

I shrug.

"You" – she grins – "just need a muse. Follow me." She grabs my hand.

"Um, have we met?" I ask as she drags me up a hill.

"Typical Pom, all handshakes and intros!" She folds her arms. "OK, who are you? But" – she places a finger on my lips – "I don't care what your parents named their screaming baby. Who are *you*?"

I blink. "I don't understand."

"I don't know you and you don't know me." She smiles, tucking a stray curl behind her ear. "We can be whoever we want to be. So who are you?"

No pressure. A million names crowd my head.

Brad? Too American. Sean? That's a fricking sheep. Hugo? A kid's film.

"Maybe I should choose for you."

I cringe inwardly as her dark eyes slide slowly over my body. What do I look like to this goddess? A nerd? A pasty Brit? I brace myself for her choice. Nigel? Worse? Graham?

Suddenly she nods decisively. "Romeo."

My eyebrows shoot upwards.

She shrugs. "He wrote terrible poetry too."

I grin. "And who are you?"

"Juliet. *Bien sûr.*"

"*Bien sûr.*" I smile.

As we emerge from the trees, I find myself staring up at a crumbling tower on the cliff edge. "What is this place?" I ask.

"This" – Juliet strokes the peachy stones – "is Myrianthe's castle. She was a Greek princess who fell in love with a servant, Stefan. Her furious father shipped Stefan to Crete, hoping Myrianthe would forget him. But she never did. She moved into this tower, forever gazing across the waves that parted them, waiting for her lost love to return."

"And did he?"

Juliet sighs. "No."

"Bummer."

"But then Aphrodite took pity on Myrianthe. She told her to jump out of her window, and she would be reunited with her lover."

"What, in the *afterlife*?" I stare up at the window, with its sheer drop into the gushing waves far below.

Juliet smiles. "Aphrodite promised that if Myrianthe took a leap of faith, love would be her reward. So she jumped. And the instant her feet left the windowsill, Myrianthe turned into a beautiful white bird, so she could fly across the sea to her long-lost love."

"Cool."

"But what she didn't know was that Poseidon had also taken pity on Stefan, and had at that very moment turned him into a dolphin, so he could swim home to Myrianthe."

"Bugger."

"But that didn't stop the star-crossed lovers. They found each other, and, determined to be together, the bird learned to swim in the sea and the dolphin learned to leap high into the sky, and they lived in the ocean together forever more. Romantic, huh?"

I nod. "If you don't mind having freaky mutant kids!"

She laughs, her eyes following a seagull as it soars effortlessly above us. "Don't you wish you were a bird? That you could just take off and fly away whenever you want, wherever you want?"

I shake my head. "I'm scared of heights."

"Scared of heights, or scared of falling?"

"Falling, I guess. From heights."

"You should do something that scares you every day." She smiles. "It's the only way you know you're alive. Come on."

"Where are we going?"

"Follow me." She winks, then turns and sprints towards the cliff edge, and before I can stop her, she dives off.

I race to the edge, heart pounding, as she plummets head first into the sea, her long brown legs disappearing in a circle of white froth.

"Juliet!" I yell. *"Juliet!"*

Suddenly she bobs to the surface.

"Are you *mental*?" I yell down at her, dizzy with relief. "You could've been killed!"

"At least I'd have died living!" She laughs. "Come on in – the water's beautiful."

"No way." I step back.

"Come on! Take a leap of faith, Romeo." Suddenly she winces. "Ow!"

I frown. "Are you OK?"

"No!" she cries. "Cramp. I can't swim!"

Shit! "Hold on – I'll get help!"

"No time! Help me, Romeo! Jump!"

Jump?! My knees tremble at the thought but I swallow hard. *I can do this. Just don't look down. Don't look down.*

I look down. Bugger, it's a long way!

I back away from the edge, take a deep breath, run up, jump – then OH BLEEDING BUGGERING

BALLS, *WHERE'S THE BLOODY SEA?* My arms flail like spaghetti and a ridiculously girly scream rips from my throat as the water rushes up to meet me and I smash into the waves.

I'm drowning! There's nothing but dark sea everywhere. Which way's up?

Somehow my head breaks the surface and I gasp for air, lungs bursting, seawater stinging my eyes as adrenalin floods my veins.

"Juliet!" I stare around desperately at the empty sea. "Where are you? *Juliet!*"

"Here!"

I twist round and she bobs up in front of me.

"Are you OK?!"

"Never better." She grins. "You?"

"What? But—"

She stops my mouth with her lips, and as she kisses me I find myself drowning all over again.

That night, I lie awake, convinced that I invented her – that I fell asleep on the beach and dreamed up a golden-skinned goddess who called me Romeo and persuaded me to jump off a cliff. That sort of thing doesn't happen in real life. I've been reading too much Shakespeare; spent too long in the sun. Now I'm even imagining taps at my window. On the first floor. Sunstroke, for sure.

"Romeo!"

My eyes fly open.

"Romeo!"

I roll over.

"Where are you, Romeo?"

I open the window. *"Juliet?"*

"Hi." She grins at me from the balcony. "Whatcha doing?"

What am *I* doing? "Uh, sleeping?"

She rolls her eyes. "We can sleep when we're dead."

"Wait – how did you ... you climbed a *tree*?" I stare as she gingerly climbs back onto the branch.

"Didn't want to wake your folks," she whispers. "But it's gonna be harder getting back down."

"Well, use the stairs."

"Where's the fun in that?" She winks. "You hungry?"

"You're cute when you're worried." Juliet grins, tracing her fingers over my forehead as the waiter pours champagne into our glasses at a little taverna on the harbour. "You get all these little lines."

"Juliet, I haven't – I mean…" I lower my voice. "I don't think I've got enough money on me for—"

"Relax." Her finger silences my lips. "It's fine. I hope you like lobster – I pre-ordered."

"But—"

"Trust me." She tilts her head. "Just enjoy, OK?"

"OK…" I say uncertainly.

"Oops, there's more lines." She leans forward, her warm breath making goosebumps prickle all the way down my neck as she kisses me. "They're irresistible."

The lobster is incredible and the champagne is cold and bubbly and delicious, but it takes three glassfuls before I pluck up enough courage to ask the question that's been bothering me.

"Juliet..." I hesitate. "Why me?"

"Huh?"

"I mean ... there were heaps of guys on the beach today – bronzed, buffed blokes – so why choose me?"

She laughs. "Why not you?"

"I mean – seriously. I'm just..." I shrug.

"We know what we are, but know not what we may be." She shrugs back. "We've all got untapped potential. Hidden talents. We don't know what we're really capable of till we're put to the test." She grins. "I can't believe you jumped off that cliff for me. I bet you didn't even think you could do it."

"I was conned," I argue. "I *thought* you were drowning."

"But do you regret it?" She raises an eyebrow.

I grin. "No way."

"Exactly. We waste so much time being afraid." She raises her glass. *"Carpe diem!"*

"Carpe diem!" I smile.

"Now run."

"What?"

"Run!"

She leaps from her chair, grabs my hand and sprints out of the restaurant, dragging me, stumbling, behind her.

"Hey!" A burly Greek waiter yells after us. "Stop!" He knocks over a table as he gives chase.

"He's gaining on us!" I cry as we race along the harbour.

"Come on!" Juliet shrieks, kicking off her shoes and sprinting towards the edge.

"What?" Not again!

"Jump!" she squeals, leaping into the sea.

So I do. The water engulfs me, colder now, as I swim as hard as I can, the waiter left gesticulating angrily on the marina.

We don't stop swimming till we reach a rocky cove.

"Why is it" – I gasp for breath – "that whenever I'm with you, I end up soaking wet?"

She giggles.

"You're crazy!" I laugh. "You're certifiably— Oh my God, Juliet – you're glowing!"

Her entire body is surrounded in a glimmering blue halo. She grins. "Magical, huh?" She looks like a mermaid. Or a siren. Or Mystique from *X-Men*. "You're doing it too."

"What is it? Radioactive seawater?"

"Plankton. They light up when they're disturbed." She sweeps her arms through the water and a million blue sparks ignite.

"It's beautiful."

"Yup. It's meant to attract their predators' predators. Like sharks."

"Sharks?" I spin around quickly.

She laughs, splashing me with cascades of turquoise crystals. "You're such a dork!"

"Oh, really?" I splash her back, and as she retaliates the sea erupts like a blue volcano.

"OK! Truce! Truce!" I laugh, wiping seawater from my eyes. "Ouch! They kinda prickle on my arms."

"That's because they're trapped under your

clothes," Juliet says. "You should take them off."

"What?"

She pulls her dress over her head in one smooth move, sprinkling blue diamonds all around as she flings it onto a nearby rock.

Wow. OK. Wow. The plankton stick to her skin, her curves glowing blue and ethereal in the dark water, and I have no idea where to look.

Face. Concentrate on her face.

"Your turn."

My fingers fumble on my slippery shirt buttons.

"Relax," she murmurs, swimming closer. "Don't be scared."

"I'm not scared." Nervous. Embarrassed. Painfully self-conscious, yes. Scared? Hell, yes. But part of me is excited too.

Bet you can guess which part.

Slowly she unbuttons my shirt, tugs it off, and tosses it onto the rock. Her hands move to my belt buckle and she hesitates.

"You OK?" I ask softly.

She nods. "Just … it's not like I go

skinny-dipping every night, you know? Or, like, ever."

"No?" I smile, flooded with surprised relief. I cup her face, her cheeks blushing hot against my palms as I kiss her gently.

And suddenly I'm not scared at all.

Moonlight glimmers on our skin as we lie on the smooth, flat rock, curled round each other so I can hardly tell what's her and what's me in the darkness.

"Are you awake?" I whisper into her hair.

"Yes. Why are we whispering?"

"Don't know." I smile, brushing a hair off her neck and kissing it gently. "It feels right." I trace a silvery-white line behind her ear. "What's this?"

She sighs. "I had an operation a while ago."

"Was it serious?"

She shrugs. "It made me realize that you should seize every moment and just squeeze every last drop right out of it, you know? Shoot for the stars."

I gaze up at the glittering sky. "I've never seen so many."

"I think there are more here than anywhere else." She sighs. "I love this island. I used to come here every summer – I even saw a falling star once." She smiles. "Grandpa told me to put it in my pocket – you know, like the song?"

"I *love* that song."

"You know, songs are just poems put to music. You should write a song for your assignment instead. You could write about the stars, or the island." She sighs again. "I can't believe this is my last summer here."

I frown. "How come?"

She shrugs. "Grandpa's gone, and I'm ... not a little girl any more. Nothing lasts forever..."

"Except the stars." I smile, looking up. "They're always there."

She shakes her head. "Most of them are gone already."

I frown. "What do you mean?"

"The stars are millions of trillions of miles away. It takes so long for their light to reach us that most of them have died before we ever see them."

"That's so sad."

"No, it's magical." She smiles, her face pale in the moonlight. "They're gone, but they still get to live on in our eyes. Grandpa used to tell me their names, but I could never remember. There are just too many."

"Well" – I point over her shoulder – "that saucepan-shaped one is the Plough, and those three stars in a row are Orion's Belt." I kiss her scar. "What star sign are you?"

"Dunno. My birthday's the twelfth of July."

"So you're Cancer, the crab."

"Do you believe in star signs?" Juliet asks quietly, her eyes clouding. "That our future is written in the stars?"

I shrug. "Who knows?"

"Romeo and Juliet's was, I guess." She hugs herself. "They were star-crossed lovers. Like us."

"No." I turn her to face me. "Not like us. Romeo and Juliet suffered from a fatal lack of communication, that's all."

She laughs. "You reckon?"

"Uh-huh. We, on the other hand – though inconveniently residing on opposite sides of the globe – live in the age of texts, Twitter and emails."

"Yeah, but you forget – your writing really sucks!"

"Ah, but *you* forget" – I stroke her cheek – "now I've found my muse."

"You don't even know me."

"I do. I know that your nose crinkles when you smile."

She smiles.

"I know that you miss your grandpa."

She nods.

"I know that you're a complete adrenalin junkie who finds absolutely any excuse to swim fully clothed. Or not."

She laughs.

"I know there's a million things I don't know about you. I don't even know your name. But I know that I want to find them out. That I don't want this night to end."

"That makes two of us."

"Looks like the sun has other ideas, though." I sigh.

"What?" She turns to face the brightening horizon and her face falls. "I've got to go." She scrambles to her feet.

"Wait – I'll walk you home—"

"No," she says quickly, wriggling into her damp dress. "I'll be fine. Thank you." She kisses me. "'Parting is such sweet sorrow, That I shall say good night...'"

"'Till it be morrow.'" I smile. "Meet me in the morning."

She hesitates, so I catch her hand. "At Myrianthe's castle. Ten a.m."

She squeezes my hand. "I'd love to." She kisses me again, more fiercely than ever, then she dives into the sea of stars, trailing the swirling galaxies glittering behind her.

But by 10.45 a.m. there's still no sign of Juliet. The day stretches, my eyes glued to the pathway from the woods, and I feel like Myrianthe, waiting. Except her lover never came. I swallow hard and check my watch for the hundredth time. Maybe something's wrong; something's happened. I can't even go looking for her – I don't even know her real name...

Restless, I wander back into the woods and meet an old woman trudging up the hill. "Have you seen a girl?" I ask her quickly. "About eighteen, long dark curly hair?"

"You're Romeo?" she says.

"Yes! Is she all right? She was meant to meet me at Myrianthe's castle."

"Where?"

"Myrianthe's castle – here."

"Oh, the old lighthouse."

I frown.

"I have a letter for you." She passes me a folded sheet of paper.

Dear Romeo,
By the time you read this I'll be gone.
I'm so sorry to leave without seeing you,
but I hate goodbyes.

Thank you so much for making my last
summer here so perfect.
Your
Juliet xx

I frown. "She's gone?"

The woman nods.

"I can't believe it." I crumple the letter in my
fist. So much for love.

"No!" The old woman grabs my arm. "Don't
be angry."

"I didn't mean anything to her," I say bitterly.
"There's no phone number, no email—"

"There's no point," the woman says quietly.

"What?" For the first time, I notice the tears
shining in her eyes.

"She's sick ... of goodbyes." She frowns, her
voice cracking. "There have been far too many."

I stare at her, at the terrible, achingly sad look
on her face, and I can hardly breathe. "What? But
she never..." I falter. "I didn't..." I glance down
at her note and suddenly all the things Juliet said

come back to me with a whole new meaning.

Her last summer...

Her scar gleaming in the moonlight. The operation that gave her a new hunger for life.

"You should seize every moment and just squeeze every last drop right out of it."

"At least I'd have died living!"

"We can sleep when we're dead."

But most of all the way her eyes clouded when I told her her star sign.

Cancer.

I swallow the tears scorching my throat. "But I ... I don't even know her name."

"It's—"

"No," I say quickly. "Don't tell me. She's Juliet. To me, she'll always be Juliet."

The old lady nods. "She'd like that."

I close my eyes and instantly Juliet's beaming face fills my head, those eyes sparkling in the moonlight as she glowed with the light of a thousand stars.

When I open them again, the woman is gone. Slowly I wander back to the tower – or lighthouse, or whatever – and sit down on the grassy clifftop. The seagulls wheel carelessly overhead and I watch the empty waves for what seems like forever. Then I pick up my pen.

Star-Crossed (lyrics)

I only knew you for a day;
You said our love was cursed
Like Romeo and Juliet,
Ill-fated from the first.

You taught me how to live and love,
To dive straight in, head first;
To make each single second count,
For life can't be rehearsed.

No sighs, no lies, no long goodbyes,
Our bubble never burst.
You were, and are – will always be –
The girl that I loved first.

Just twenty-four short fleeting hours,
Our time was brief, it's true.
But my life was changed forever
By one day of loving you.

SUPERCOOL

Cathy Kelly

Cool gangs run schools. It's a law. The Law of Coolness. Like the laws in chemistry and maths, only easier to understand than anything to do with isosceles triangles or the periodic table. If you are cool, you get to ignore people or make them popular simply by inviting them to join the gang. I need not point out at this stage that I am not a Cool Person. You will have figured that out by now. I don't want to be one, either – not if it means being *that* sort of girl.

I wouldn't mind being cool in a sort of general, casually chic way, but I would not want to be one of the Cool People in my new school, Laurence O'Toole Tech, because the local version of cool is a horrible, vampiric, life-draining type of behaviour without any of the nicer, softer characteristics of vampires. I mean, vampires don't *play* with their prey, do they?

But sometimes, just sometimes, the Cool People lose. And the Uncool People get to fall in love.

My first day in Laurence O'Toole Tech made me feel sick. That was before I even got there.

At breakfast that morning, I honestly couldn't say, "Mum, I feel sick," because my mother was already upset enough about us having to move from our house in Sycamore Avenue, where we had lived since before I was born, to a tiny bungalow five miles away – which meant I had to move schools. The recession sucks, is all I'll say.

When we moved house during the summer, Mum cried a lot. She cries nicely, so she looks pretty, just with wet skin. I do not take after her. I cry and instantly turn into human strawberry jelly: red, blubbery, ugly.

I hate it when Mum cries. It just feels *wrong*.

"I'm so sorry, Izzie," she said the day she and Dad told me just how broke we were. "You'll have to leave all your friends, your school, and you'll have to leave Susie."

Susie's my best friend (BFF if you're ten, or the person who carries all your secrets around with her if you're fifteen, like me).

"Mum, everything's going to be fine!" I said sternly, trying to sound like a movie heroine when she and the hero are about to face a firing squad/ alien encounter/whatever. "We're a strong family; we can take it."

This type of statement makes grown-ups remember that they *are* the grown-ups and then they stop crying. If you are being brave, then they can be brave.

I hugged Mum. Our dog, Rua, jumped onto my dad's lap then and bounced around happily, wagging his tail with his tongue hanging out. Rua thinks everything is a game. He was definitely dropped on his head as a puppy.

"So what if we have to move? It might be fun

to start new lives somewhere else," I added.

I really am a brilliant liar.

After that speech, I simply couldn't have told Mum and Dad that I felt sick and didn't want to go to my new school.

I definitely *looked* sick, though. My new uniform was a burgundy skirt and jumper with a white shirt, and tie. White doesn't suit me because my hair is black and my skin is on the cool side of blue. Combined with the burgundy, it made me look like the undead.

Or a goth – whichever is worse.

Mum made pancakes for me for breakfast. Since she lost her job, she cooks a lot, and this is lovely when it's cakes on Saturday – but not so lovely when your stomach is doing cartwheels of worry and you are expected to eat two huge pancakes.

"Thanks," I said, still cheery.

I had said it was going to be fun and I was not going to let them all down. IT WOULD BE FUN!

♥ ♥ ♥

The thing is, I had this instinct that it *wasn't* going to be fun.

Nobody at Laurence O'Toole Tech had wanted me to come in a day early for orientation, which seemed odd to me. In my old school, the head nun would have dragged any new pupils in a week early. She'd have shown them every square inch of the place, including the tampon machine in the upper-floor bathroom of which she was very proud (I don't think they have one in the convent), and told them her door was always open. Mum and I drove past Laurence O'Toole last week, but that was as close as I'd got. (I do miss Sister Mary-Louise. She was totally mental, but in a nice way.)

Mum insisted on driving me to school that morning because it's a fifteen-minute walk. Plus, she wanted to wave goodbye, possibly even see the classrooms – which is the sort of thing Sister Mary-Louise would have encouraged.

When we arrived, pupils were sullenly marching in on the first day back after the summer holidays and I had another of those sick feelings.

This one said it would not be a good plan for Mum to come inside. Only the smallest of kids were being dropped off by parents, and even they were flinging themselves from the cars at high speed, because they knew that parental lifts would get you jeered at in the playground.

"Mum, I'd like to go in on my own," I told her and hugged her.

Mum bit her lip, so I turned off the radio and turned on the CD player until *Glee Four* was belting out of the car. You can't feel sad to *Glee*, can you?

I threw myself from the car and began the death march up to the gates. The Laurence O'Toole architect had obviously been in an industrial-wasteland-sort-of-mood when he drew the plans for it. Everything was grey, even the grass.

"Cheery," I muttered to myself.

Inside, the building was grey with paler grey highlights and red stripes on the floor that looked like those ones you see on documentaries about prisons. *Follow the red line. Do not move suddenly or the guards will shoot you.* There were lots of prison-style signs with directions, so I found the registration office OK. But it took ages to check in with the nervy young guy on the reception desk who didn't look old enough to be a teacher. He handed me a class timetable based on the subjects I'd been doing at my old school and gave me a very chunky printout on "Forbidden Behaviour". *(No make-up is to be worn. Do not write in spray paint on the walls. No piercings allowed other than earrings.)*

I smiled at him, asked for a map of the school and then headed off to my first class, which was a meeting of my entire year in the fourth-year form room.

Due to going to registration, I was the last person to arrive. There were at least sixty people there, some squashed up against the walls, with the sweet nerdy kids sitting at the front, looking up at the teacher, pens or laptops at the ready. At the back, lined up like sharks, were the bad kids. None of them was obeying the piercing rule, that was for sure. Among the sharks was a cluster of girls so glossy and lovely that they looked as if they'd been beamed straight down from an *America's Next Top Model* shoot. Their make-up was perfect, their hair rippled in honey blondes or lush chestnuts. Their school uniforms had been subtly altered to look almost fashionable, which was a miracle in itself.

Yes, they were the Cool People.

I shuffled into the room and leaned against a wall while everybody in the whole room eyeballed me. I knew what they were seeing:

My eyes are such a dark brown that they're nearly black, and my best friend, Susie, always complains that I never need eyeliner or mascara as I look as if I'm wearing eye make-up anyway. I do not tan, so I don't bother trying, and among a load of kids with golden tans from the summer, I looked like a total goth-head who'd been shipped in from Alaska. I am also tall for my age. You get the picture: the Strange New Girl.

I eyeballed them all right back anyway. Show No Fear is the best bet.

And then I saw him, lounging against the window nearest to the teacher. At that moment, all the other people: cool girls, nerdy kids, huge sporty guys, *everyone*, seemed to disappear. The drone of the teacher telling us about the year ahead and what was expected of us disappeared too.

We stared at each other across the classroom.

I stopped worrying if I was too tall, too pale or too spikily different to the other girls.

Instead, I stared into eyes that looked as dark as my own and a face that said this guy thought, imagined, had *dreams* of a life outside Laurence O'Toole Tech.

He was just as tall and strong as the super-sporty jocks, but his face, with the dark hair swept low over his brows, said he liked the library, wrote poetry and would be kind to little kids. I instinctively knew he would play guitar with those long, strong fingers. He wasn't pale like me. He was the colour of sun-baked caramel, and he was so handsome that I felt something inside me, well ... *flip*. I know that sounds insane.

Who knew bits of you could actually flip?

Nothing inside me had ever moved in any meaningful way for any other guy before, although I'd had a moment once with my first boyfriend – but that was more a locking of braces, and it was a relieved flip that we weren't stuck together permanently.

This guy, staring across the fourth-year class-room, was the One.

Fifteen minutes into lunchtime, I was tripped up by a Top Model, who stuck her foot out when I passed her in the canteen queue with my full lunch tray as I was looking for somewhere to plonk myself.

"Sorry," she said insincerely, flicking back her hair (blonde) and smirking as everyone else in her gang laughed out loud.

"Amelia, what are you like!" Somebody be-hind her in the queue laughed.

My lunch was all over the floor, I had landed painfully on my knees and for the second time that day, everyone in a room was staring at me.

I looked up in time to see one of the Glossy-Hair Brigade nudge Amelia and point. "Jake's looking over at you," she hissed.

In my dazed state, I looked in the direction she was pointing and saw Him, with his gang, his dark hair even more ruffled and his shirt's top button open, his school tie loose. He was staring intently at us and I felt myself go pink with embarrassment.

He smiled suddenly and I smiled back. I couldn't help it. That little flip in my stomach happened again, and I knew I was probably looking at him goofily. I didn't care. Until Amelia caught sight of my smile.

"He's not smiling at *you*, moron," she snapped. "How stupid can you be? Jake is so out of your league, he's on a different planet. Your planet is Planet Dork, by the way."

And she moved further down the queue, grinding my blueberry muffin into the canteen floor as she went.

Don't cry, I told myself as I tidied up, feeling every eye still on me. Nobody came to help. They would have in my old school. But then nobody in my old school would have got away with the sort of blatant bullying Amelia had just displayed.

I threw what was left of my lunch in the bin and headed to the library. I still wanted to cry, but I knew it would be fatal to do it in public. If this place was Bullying Central, then I needed to lick my wounds in private.

In the library, I found one of those pony books I used to love when I was little. Knowing it would cheer me up, I read it till the end-of-lunch bell. There were quite a few other students in the library – they all looked as if they were used to making themselves as unnoticed as possible, which was probably the way to go in this school. A few of them smiled nervously at me and I nodded back. We were like inmates in a nasty prison.

"How was it?" Mum was eager and worried in equal measure when I got home.

I'd spent the walk home exercising my smiling muscles, so that I could summon up a big beam when I saw her. "Great," I said. "Big, you know. It might take some time to get used to the size of the place, but it's nice."

I might enter myself into the lying event in the Olympics.

"Darling, that's wonderful," she said, and hugged me, clearly letting go of a whole day's worth of anxiety. "I texted, but when you didn't text back, I figured you weren't allowed to use your phone."

"Absolutely not," I said. "Lots of rules – which everyone obeys." Another lie. Gold in the Olympics, for sure. "I've tons of homework," I added – which was not a lie.

I dragged Rua upstairs with me, shut my bedroom door, then curled up on the bed with him and sobbed. Rua is great for this type of thing: he licks your tears away and doesn't mind when you squeeze him tightly in misery. I listened to Lady Gaga and imagined a world where I dressed in lethal leather and karate-kicked Amelia and her hench-girls to the kerb.

♥ ♥ ♥

Day Two and I had a new strategy. Since nobody else was following the no-make-up rule, I used my Mac eye-shadow kit to give me Lethal-Karate-Girl eyes and took my biker boots out of hibernation. With my skirt hitched up a bit, holey black opaque tights, the boots and my hair straight, I certainly looked cool – and the precise opposite of Amelia. I was Tough Cookie to her Golden Girl.

"You're not going to school dressed like that?" Dad looked a little shocked when I stalked into the kitchen. (You've got to practise things like stalking – get yourself into the zone, you know.)

I toyed with the idea of telling Dad the truth and explaining that if I was dressed to kill I would feel more "Warrior Girl" and so more ready to take on the bullies. I didn't want to worry him or Mum, though, so I smiled and said, "It's a dress-up day today, Dad. Fun, huh?"

I just hoped he'd have enough money to bail me out when I was arrested for stabbing Amelia in the bum with my protractor – but I didn't mention this. The stabbing-her-in-the-bum plan was only if she got physical with me again. Last resort sort of stuff.

"I'll walk to school, Mum," I said. "I need the exercise and it'll wake me up."

I'd been awake since six with nerves, but there was no point telling her this. I was stuck with Laurence O'Toole Tech, so I needed to learn how to cope with it.

On the way to school, I phoned Susie.

"You never rang last night," she said instantly. "Was it that bad?"

"Worse," I said and told her everything.

"The bitch," she hissed.

There is something utterly comforting about talking to a friend who loves and understands you totally. Susie has known me since we were four. She knows I'm a total softy who cries at animal cruelty programmes on the TV. She was with me the day I gave all the money in my purse to a blind guy with a whippet begging on the side of the street because it was Christmas and I couldn't bear to think of him and his lovely dog being poor and unhappy.

Suddenly, I wanted to sob my eyes out.

"No tears," Susie commanded. "She will sense fear. She will destroy you if she senses fear. Think of something nice every time you see her face."

"Yeah," I muttered and then, out of nowhere, came a vision of Him.

Tall and lean, with dark eyes that searched for me in the vast school. He was out of my league, according to Amelia, but I hadn't imagined that moment between us yesterday. Jake had looked right at me. I hadn't imagined that electric current between us either. No way.

At that moment, I stopped wanting to cry.

"Thing is," I said to Susie, "everything's not terrible. There's this guy..."

Jake was in none of my classes that morning, but Amelia was. She glared at me as I walked into the classroom for my first lesson, and if I hadn't practised my stalking earlier, I was sure I'd have wobbled a bit as I passed her desk. Somehow, I found a free seat beside a mousy-haired girl and got my textbook onto the desk without my hands shaking too much.

From this vantage point, I could see Amelia whispering something to a pretty, very curvy girl sitting near her. I knew from the curl of Amelia's pink lips that she was being nasty, and sure enough, the other girl turned away with a telltale glitter of tears in her eyes.

"What exactly *is* Amelia's problem?" I asked the mousy-haired girl beside me.

"No idea. She's always been like that. Cos she's beautiful, she gets away with it."

I didn't agree with the beautiful bit, that was for sure. Amelia has serious boobs, big blue eyes, and hair that spends lots of its time getting bleached, but she is hardly a Hollywood movie star. Her looks are all down to sheer effort. I've heard that really kind people can radiate goodness and light. Amelia radiates spite. She is pretty to look at but, like a fairy-tale creature that turns evil when the moon goes in, underneath the smile and the make-up is something vicious.

The mousy-haired girl turned towards me. She had the loveliest blue eyes, like cornflowers, and a great smile. "I'm Fiona."

"Izzie," I said, smiling back at her.

"Oh, I know," Fiona said. "You're hot gossip at the moment."

"Me?" I was surprised. There were other new kids in fourth year and I didn't think I stood out that much.

"Amelia has it in for you," Fiona informed me.

My heart didn't exactly sink, but it didn't feel bouncy with joy either.

"Why?" I asked. "I've done nothing to her. She's the one who tripped me up in the canteen yesterday. I hope this place has an anti-bullying policy, because if she does anything like that again, I'll report her – after I've paid her back."

My words sounded a lot tougher than I felt. I didn't know if I was up to dealing with a person like Amelia.

"She hates you because Jake Ryan, the hottest

guy in the entire school, told his friends that you were pretty."

"Jake said I was pretty?" I asked, dazed.

"Don't go all girly on me," said Fiona in exasperation. "Amelia's nuts about Jake, and he's never so much as looked at *her*, no matter how hard she tries – so if he likes you even a teeny bit, she'll make your life a misery, Izzie. Don't you understand?"

I didn't care.

Let Amelia launch surface-to-air missiles at me. My shield of happiness about Jake would deflect them.

Fiona was a fabulous source of school gossip, and she said that Jake did art, which was one of that afternoon's scheduled classes. "Amelia doesn't do art," she added, "so you and Jake can gaze into each other's eyes in peace."

I put on lipgloss for art and got there early – to find Jake and another guy putting chairs into a circle around one single chair. Jake looked up when I came in, and that slow, gentle smile lit up his face. His gaze made me feel warm, as though a slow heat was travelling through me. And the flipping – oh, wow, the *flipping*. My stomach was doing somersaults.

I was staring at him, and that would have made me from Planet Dork, as Amelia put it – except that he was staring back at me.

"Do you play guitar, by any chance?" I asked, before my brain had properly engaged. "It's just your fingers are so long..." Oh God, what did I just say?! I went pink, which doesn't suit me because of the white skin.

"How did you know I play guitar?" he asked softly.

My brain, having done its spectacularly dumb thing, then went into "sleep" mode, and all I could do was smile at him goofily.

He smiled back and was, *I think*, about to say something – when the rest of the class came into the room.

I floated away to a desk to sit and pretend to

attempt a life drawing of a bored-looking guy in his school uniform.

"Obviously," droned the art teacher, "life drawing is supposed to be of a nude model, but we can't manage that here."

Some people giggled, and there were a few rude remarks about nude drawings, but I just stared at my paper and sometimes at Jake, who was always looking back at me.

I have never had this happen to me before, I ought to point out. It made me almost dizzy with excitement. All my fears about the new school, new house, even the thought of horrible Amelia, faded blissfully into the background.

As I sketched, badly, I was immersed in a fantasy world where Jake and I were lying on the grass in the park and looking up at the clouds, trying to work out what shapes they resembled. I've always wanted to do that with a boyfriend.

As we left art, Jake moved closer to me and touched my hand. I thought he would speak again, but then we were separated in the crowd.

I floated through history and even managed to cope with my first chemistry lesson with Ms Carter, who has grey, sticky-up hair and a total disregard for colour when it comes to clothes. (People over nineteen shouldn't be allowed to wear neon T-shirts.) "She's a bit eccentric," I muttered to Fiona, who I'd managed to sit beside again.

"Mad," was Fiona's one-word reply.

The final bell rang, and the entire school erupted into the halls for the frantic rush to lockers and bags. Fiona and I reached the locker hall to see Amelia's gang surrounding a couple of what had to be first-years – small girls who looked like bush babies with their big, startled eyes. My best friend, Susie, has a twelve-year-old sister, Jennie, who's in first year, and they all reminded me of her: sweet, inquisitive and dying to belong to "big" school.

Amelia's gang didn't look like they shared my fondness for younger kids. People were generally keeping out of the way, as if everyone had decided that avoiding the gang was the best bet.

"I *didn't* have an iPhone Five," Amelia was hissing to a dark-haired girl with shiny black Mary Jane shoes and a look of innocence that had marked her as a likely victim from the start. "But I do now!" Smiling, Amelia snatched the phone from the smaller girl's shaking hand. The cover was pink and sparkly and, with one practiced move, Amelia ripped it off.

Perhaps it was to do with my Karate-Warrior Girl outfit, but something inside me snapped. Of course, there had been bullying in my other school – there is bullying everywhere – but the teachers had always stamped it out quickly. We were a "telling school", Sister Mary-Louise explained. If we saw someone being bullied, we told a teacher. There was no rubbish about not telling on people you knew. "Zero tolerance", Sister Mary-Louise had called it grimly.

I wanted zero tolerance here too. How dare Amelia pick on little kids?

Ignoring Fiona's shout of "Don't, Izzie!", I stalked up to the group. I grabbed Amelia and forcefully whirled her round till she was facing me. I ripped the phone from her hands. "Don't pick on smaller kids," I snarled. I leaned forward, and down – suddenly realizing I was taller than her. "Don't pick on anyone, in fact."

Before Amelia could manage to reply, I grabbed her jumper and pulled her in the direction of the admin office. In case you think I was being too tough, this girl had been terrorizing people for years. The time had come for desperate measures. Besides, dragging her was the only way I thought I'd get her there.

I must have really been channelling the Warrior Girl because I felt so strong. "Coming?" I roared to the crowd behind me.

Nobody replied.

"Don't be such cowards," said Fiona, bravely pushing through a few of Amelia's shocked gang to stand beside me.

"Let go of me, you bitch!" shrieked Amelia. She was properly struggling now.

But you can't struggle successfully in

fashionable heels. I was taller, stronger, and I was wearing my trusty biker boots. Plus, Amelia stood for everything I hated, which made me weirdly strong.

"You don't get to pick on the smaller kids with me around," I said to her. "Let's see what the principal has to say about this."

Since I didn't really know where the principal's office was, I didn't know where to go and paused for a moment to think. Amelia was struggling like crazy. I wouldn't be able to hold onto her much longer.

"Let her go!" one of her gang yelled.

"Hold onto her," said a male voice.

Stalking down the corridor was Jake.

"Jake!" the small first-year in the Mary Jane shoes cried, and she ran into his arms.

He hugged her, whispered into her ear and then marched up to us. "Did you steal my little sister's phone, Amelia?" he said in that low voice that wasn't soft now. It was diamond hard.

"I didn't know she was your sister," pleaded

Amelia, suddenly broken. After all, bullying the little sister of the guy you fancy is not a good *lurve* move.

"You shouldn't bully anyone," he said, giving her such a look of acid dislike that I was surprised her make-up didn't start dripping down her face.

Amelia knew she was beaten.

Afterwards, everyone wanted to talk about it. But I just wanted to go home. Now that it was over, I was too shaken by Amelia's cruelty and by how Jake hadn't even looked at me when he said thanks for saving his little sister.

Susie and I talked on the phone for an hour that night, going over everything in detail. "You're a heroine, Izzie," Susie said. "Be proud of yourself for what you did."

"I am..." I began. But I felt sad too. I must have imagined that Jake felt something for me, otherwise he'd have looked at me or hugged me or something...

♥ ♥ ♥

The principal wanted to see me first thing the next day. Amelia had been suspended for two weeks. He said a new anti-bullying policy was being put in place and told me I had done well to try and stop the bullying, but added that dragging another student to his office was not the answer.

"I will phone your parents to tell them how you behaved," Mr McArthur said, "and explain that while we don't tolerate students physically grabbing others, you were acting in the interests of much younger children."

"So I'm not in trouble?" I asked.

The corners of Mr McArthur's stern mouth raised a fraction. "Absolutely not," he said.

First class was maths and Fiona had held a seat for me. Everyone still stared at me but a few people slapped me on the back. "You go, girl!"

"They're all talking about you," said Fiona gleefully.

"Are they?" I muttered, taking out my maths

book. The one person I wanted to talk about me, or to me, was nowhere to be seen.

Jake arrived late for maths, and one of his friends obligingly moved so he could slide into the seat next to mine. I felt as if I couldn't breathe.

He leaned over and took my hand under the desk and murmured, "Thank you, thank you, and thank you. That's from my mum and dad, and Claire, my little sister."

The flipping thing was happening again. He kissed my hand. His mouth was so soft and warm against my palm. "That's from me," he said.

I could feel him beside me the whole lesson and I couldn't concentrate on one single theorem. Not one.

"I'll tell you what homework we got." Fiona smiled, knowing that I'd missed everything the teacher had said, as Jake and I walked out of the classroom, hand in hand.

"I wanted to get your number yesterday," Jake said as soon as we were outside in the corridor.

"But there was no time and then everything happened." He handed me a piece of paper with a number on it.

I looked at the paper, dialled the number on my mobile, then hung up. "Now you have me," I said softly.

"I don't know anything about you, Izzie, but I do know you're the most amazingly brave and beautiful girl I've ever met," he said.

"Really?" I said, looking up at him.

"Really."

And then his lips brushed mine, and, well, the flipping thing went quite out of control.

The Cool People don't own the school any more. We've become sort of anti-cool – because Amelia and her gang were the cool ones and they made everyone's lives hell. There are still bullies, but they don't get so much of a chance in Laurence O'Toole any more.

As for me and Jake... Well, we lie on the grass in the park and look up at the clouds. And sometimes I can't see the clouds because he leans over and kisses me. And then I just see clouds in my head: the lovely happy clouds of a happy ending.

EXTRACURRICULARS

Abby McDonald

Let me make it clear, my life was going great until Charlie Sutton sauntered into the college library one rainy Tuesday lunchtime and turned everything upside down.

OK, not *great*, maybe, but decent. Under control.

Fine. Not *under control*, more, "hanging off the edge of control by my raggedy bitten finger-nails", but still, you get it. Jenny may have woken up one morning and decided she didn't want to be friends any more, but I was getting by on my own. I found a system, a way to make it through the day, and ninety per cent of this plan meant hiding out in the super-secret study spot I discovered in the back corner of the library.

It's perfect. Tucked way back in the classics section, far from the banks of shiny new computers and DVDs for loan and well-thumbed copies of *The Great Gatsby* and *Beloved*. There's a single study carrel sandwiched between the shelves, next to an ancient, clunky PC that still runs Windows 98 and shudders in protest if you even try to load a page with Flash (like, say, the entire modern Internet). The librarians can't see me – *nobody* can see me – nibbling my sandwiches, doing homework, killing time while Jenny lounges in the main hallway with Sascha and the rest of her shiny new Foundation Art friends.

In a few short weeks, it's become my sanctuary, my escape, my only relief in the great sprawling mess of loneliness that is the sum total of my life. It's most definitely *not* the place I want to find the resident Year-Twelve Romeo, Charlie Sutton, staring down at me with that arrogant smirk of his.

"What?" I ask shortly. "This spot's taken."

"I can see." He gazes around at the square

metre I've claimed as personal territory: the cardigan on the chair, my files in permanent residence on the desk, a water bottle and illicit snacks slipped under a magazine. "Why don't you just move in a TV and call it a day?"

I don't reply. If you ignore a problem, it goes away, right? Even if the problem is a tall, brown-haired, hoodie-wearing boy who's most often described as "Captain America's chavvy younger brother". (Like that's a good thing?!)

Charlie makes a show of leaning against the desk, like it's his personal kingdom. "Vita, Vita, Vita... It's lunch break. As in a break from work. Don't you have anywhere better to be?"

I stare at my economics textbook.

"All work and no play," he says, sing-song, until finally I snap.

"Go away!"

"Shh!" Charlie scolds me, laughing. "This is a library."

"Exactly." I glare back, lowering my voice to a hiss. "What are you even doing in here? Shouldn't you be off getting an ASBO somewhere? This is a *learning* environment."

"And I plan on getting educated." He waggles his eyebrows suggestively.

I groan. "Please tell me you're not here to meet Taysha," I say, naming his latest girlfriend of the week. Or last week. I can't keep up.

"I'm not." He leans to peer at the papers on my desk. I slam a folder down on top of them. "It's Kristii."

I form a vague mental image: blonde, tourism BTEC, eyebrows like an underfed tapeworm. "Let me guess; she spells it with an i?"

"Two of them." Charlie grins back, like he's amused. "She signs little hearts on top; it's adorable."

"I bet it is."

Charlie begins pulling books out of the stacks and reshelving them out of place, spines inward. "Enough about her; I want to know all about you."

"Sure you do." I don't even try to hide my sarcasm. Charlie Sutton has been slouched in the back of my economics class all year, and aside from the time he made a spirited argument *against* equal pay for women – "Because you're only killing time before you get knocked up, right, babe?" – he hasn't said a word to me.

"I mean it." Charlie tries the charming grin that has felled half the girls in year twelve (and, according to rumour, the gap-year student in the front office too). "What's your deal? Is this why I never see you around any more – you just hide out here all day and hope nobody finds you?"

I flush red, but before I can manage a reply, there's a bored sigh behind us. "Charlie?"

He turns. Kristii-with-two-i's is waiting, wearing a cropped peach T-shirt and floating asymmetrical pale green skirt – despite the fact that it's raining. In England. In March.

She raises one underfed eyebrow. "I have class in, like, ten minutes."

"I'm all yours, babe." Charlie turns back to me. "She's a beast!" he whispers with a wink.

I roll my eyes as he ushers Kristii off into the

next stack, and moments later, low murmurs and giggles start up.

I plug my iPod in and fix my gaze firmly back on my textbook, but I can't ignore the flush of embarrassment still in my cheeks. Charlie has one thing right: I'm an expert at hiding.

I know it's not impressive as super-powers go, but it's harder than you think. When I was younger, it was simple: all I needed was a tiny space to crawl into, a tree to climb. My favourite books were those about a group of mischievous kids who roamed around 1950s England – they were forever discovering smugglers' plots and mysterious gold shipments, or running off to live on a secret island. I would keep a packed bag with me at all times, full of essentials: pen and paper (for SOS notes); provisions (crumbled biscuits in foil); a twist-on torch (for flashing Morse code); and, of course, three more books, to pass the time while I was stowed away in the back of that shipment of priceless antiques.

Not that I had anything bad to hide from, just my rowdy older brothers, and Dad's obsession with Radio 4, and a mum who sincerely, to this very day, believes that a girl should learn how to cook her future husband's dinner before she even gets her first period.

"But what if I'm a lesbian?" I would whine, just to tease her.

"Doesn't matter." And Mum would pull the straps of my apron tighter, like the shackles of patriarchy. "Lesbians eat chapattis too."

You can see why I liked hiding.

The problem is, now I'm sixteen, it's harder to disappear. I can't fit into the cupboard under the sink, and there are no handy trees in the grounds of Central Sussex Sixth Form College for me to scramble up. Besides, it's different now: I'm not trying to keep out of sight so much as hide my feelings. Pretend like I don't care that suddenly, halfway through year twelve, I'm all alone in a sprawling school of a thousand people who have already made their groups, found their BFFs, and don't need anyone else tagging along on the edge of their crowds. I don't care that I have nobody to eat my lunch with, or hang out with during free periods; I walk around with earbuds in to drown out the unbearable silence of nobody talking to me.

And I definitely don't care about the tight, hollow bubble in my chest, like I'm on the verge of tears all day long, and it's all I can do to dig my nails into my palms and make it home again to sit in my bedroom, surrounded by magazine cut-outs and plans for a future when I don't feel so hopelessly, miserably alone.

I catch a flash of motion out of the corner of my eye: Charlie and Kristii, visible through the gap in the books. Curious, I lean back in my chair for a clearer view. They're kissing up against the stacks, hot and heavy, the way I've never kissed anyone in my life. Like it matters, like it's *necessary*. He drops his lips to her neck, hands roaming upwards and round to her front. She moves them back down. He waits a beat, kissing some more, and then slides them back up. This time, she slaps them away.

"Charlie!"

"Sorry, babe. Couldn't help myself." He gives her that grin, and sure enough, Kristii melts.

"Not here, OK?" She slides her arms around his neck again. "My 'rents are up in London Friday night; we'll have the place to ourselves."

"Are they now?" Charlie nuzzles her neck and growls playfully. She giggles, until he mock-bites her, and then she squeals in protest.

"No marks!"

He rolls his eyes, but obeys, and then they're kissing again, shifting just out of view. I lean further, further—

My chair slips. I yelp, grabbing the desk to steady myself. Charlie opens his eyes and looks at me through the gap in the bookshelves.

I freeze.

He's still kissing her: Kristii's arms are around him and he has one hand in her hair, but he's looking at me. Just looking with those grey-blue eyes, curious. Watching me watching him.

Oh God. I unfreeze, quickly turning away as

a furious blush floods my whole face. What am I doing staring at them like some kind of kiss-deprived freak? I shove my files into my bag and grab my books, rushing so fast I bash my knee on the corner of the desk. *Owwwww!* I bite back my cry and limp painfully into the aisle, but before I go, I can't help looking back at them, just once.

Charlie is still watching me, over her shoulder. He winks.

I bolt.

I don't see Charlie for the rest of the week; life continues as normal. I get up, I go to school, I hide out in the library, and if I make it home without that tight knot of loneliness in my chest consuming the whole earth, I count the day a success. My parents don't know anything has changed: as far as they're concerned, I'm still BFFs with Jenny. They haven't noticed that my mobile doesn't ring any more, or that I never stay out after school, or that I spend every weekend at home, instead of shopping down in Brighton, or sleeping over, or doing all those basic teenage-girl friendship things that I took for granted.

"It's good you're buckling down, with your exams coming up," is all my mum says when she finds me curled up in my room reading on Saturday night. "Your cousin Alon got a B in his maths A level, and look at him now." She tuts, as if Alon's wayward life running a surf school in Sydney is something to be pitied, not applauded.

But that's the point, I suppose. I'm hiding so well, nobody sees. Not my family, not my teachers, not even my former friend, whose gaze drifts past me in the hall so casually, you'd never guess we spent years clustered under the cover at sleepovers, breathlessly confiding every tiny hope and dream. That's the irony: I'm trying so hard to be invisible, when all I really want is for someone – anyone – to notice, just see that I'm here. I exist.

Well, almost anyone.

"Hey, babe."

I return to my corner of the library for a free period the next Monday to find Charlie sprawled in my seat, his battered vintage Adidas trainers up on the desk. My desk.

I tense. "What are you doing here?" Just the memory of last week – the kissing, the *watching* – is enough to make my skin flush, a nervous flutter start in my stomach.

Charlie grins, like he can tell I'm flustered. "I had a free period, thought I'd see what you're up to."

"Studying," I answer flatly, clutching my folder against my chest like armour.

"Doesn't look like study to me..." He waves my copy of *The Duke Returns*, the dog-eared romance novel I left face down on the desk. Clearing his throat dramatically, Charlie begins to read from the back cover. "'Lady Flora is content to be a spinster, watching from the sidelines of society balls. But when the rakish Duke of Sussex—'"

I snatch it from his hand, blushing. "Don't you have to meet Kristii?"

"Kristii's over." Charlie shrugs. "Too clingy."

"Remind me to send a condolence card."

Charlie laughs, and finally unfolds himself from the chair. He makes a show of it: dusting the seat down, pulling it out for me, gesturing extravagantly. Cautiously I sit.

"I like your hair like that." He flicks one of the braids I have twisted around my head. (When you have zero social life, there's a lot of time to braid.) "It's cute."

"Uh, thanks," I manage, thrown, and then there's a delicate cough behind us.

We turn. Another girl is hovering in the aisle: Lucy Henderson, from my lit class. She's shy and bookish, and blushing like she can't believe she's meeting Charlie Sutton in the library stacks.

Charlie grins at me. "Love to stay and chat, but I've got a hot date!" He drapes an arm round Lucy's shoulder and leads her into the next row, the same place he was groping Kristii just last week.

At least he's consistent.

I settle in at the desk, half listening for the telltale giggles next door, but there's silence. Not that I care. I open my economics book, as if I can block out all thought of what Charlie is doing just metres away from me, but the chapters all blur into one.

I will not look. I will not look. *I will not*—

I look.

They're up against the stacks like he was before, making out in furious, passionate breaths. I blink in shock. Shy little Lucy? Grabbing at the back of Charlie's shirt like a girl possessed? They bump up against the shelves in their enthusiasm, the books quivering, and then he comes up for air, his eyes flickering open – straight to meet mine.

I freeze, flushing, but for some reason, I don't look away this time. Neither does Charlie. Our gaze holds as Lucy kisses his neck and along the line of his jaw, oblivious to me watching from between the books, and Charlie's attention on me.

I stop breathing.

Charlie's eyes don't leave mine; slowly he smiles. Not that famous cheeky grin, but something quieter. Curious. The moment stretches, almost as if it's frozen there between us, and I feel a rush of unfamiliar emotion. Excitement. A thrill.

I slowly smile back, caught up in the heady kick of my pulse and prickle of heat on my skin. I should look away – God, I should be dying of embarrassment right now – but I'm caught; locked in the line of sight from his blue eyes to mine, wondering—

The bell sounds, jolting me out of my daze. I snap my head away, scrambling for my things and practically sprinting out of the library. I fight my way through the students heading reluctantly to class.

What was that?!

I feel a hand on my arm. "Vita!" Charlie pulls me to a stop, and then I'm staring into those eyes again. Only this time, they're just inches away.

"What?" I'm breathless, mind still fuzzy.

"You're, um, you left this." Charlie holds out a pen.

I blink. It's a cheap biro, bitten on one end. "Uh, thanks," I manage to say, taking it from him.

My fingers brush against his for a split second before I pull back, shoving the pen into my bag.

"So..." Charlie starts, then trails off. He looks as weirded out as me, his usual arrogant expression now awkward. "I..." He pauses, swallowing. "You got class now?"

I nod.

"Me too."

Another pause. I glance away, and realize for the first time that we're standing in the middle of the main foyer with people all around. People who are staring curiously at us. People like Jenny, lounging on the stairs with Sascha and their cooler-than-thou artsy friends. Sascha leans over to whisper to Jenny, looking from me to Charlie and back again.

I gulp. "I should, you know..."

"Go?" Charlie suggests, with a flicker of a smile.

"Right. Yes. That."

"See you in class." Then he's walking away, joining a group of boys as they shove and joke their way down the hall, until the crowd closes around him and he's gone.

"So what was *that* about?" Jenny's voice comes from behind me. I startle, spinning round. She's smiling, the way she used to, the way I haven't seen in months. "Since when are you friends with Charlie Sutton?"

I could say a dozen things. *Since you last spoke to me. Since you cut your hair and got that pink streak, and started sucking face with a boy whose jeans are tighter than mine. Since I stopped mattering.*

But I don't. I shrug vaguely, about to answer when Sascha barges in, her armfuls of silver bangles clattering as she tugs Jenny's hand. "We have to get to class. Darkroom sign-up, remember?"

Jenny makes a face. "Crapsticks. Gotta run. See you!" And then they're gone too, and I'm left alone.

After that, things get … awkward. Despite the fact I've spent half a year at this school barely registering Charlie's presence, suddenly he's all I see – and no matter how hard I try, I can't *un*-notice him. How he swaggers around college, so confident and nonchalant. The fact he's got everyone – from the staff, right down to the snobby popular girls – all wrapped around his little finger. The way his vintage Manchester United shirt sort of *clings* to his body. The way he never, not once, looks as if he's lonely. Not that he'd have a chance, given the number of girls practically ripping each other's earrings out for a place on his hook-up calendar.

I try my best to avoid him. I even surrender my library hideout, and make do with loitering in empty classrooms during lunch, and out on the hill by the sports field – armed with a book and my earbuds and an expression that I hope screams "mysterious loner" more than "pathetic reject". But by Friday lunchtime I'm back in my familiar carrel, and Charlie Sutton is the last thing on my mind.

I have more important things to hide from.

"Hey, babe." Charlie appears between the stacks. "Haven't seen you all week. Miss me?" He straddles a chair, scooting in close to me.

"Sure." I manage a faint smile. "I cried into my pillow every night."

"That's what I like to hear." He reaches over, scooping a finger of icing from the single cupcake on my desk. "Fancy. What is it, your birthday or something?"

I don't reply.

His eyes widen. "Oh, shit, really? Congrats. You doing anything fun?"

I give him a look. "Does it look like I'm doing anything fun?"

Charlie doesn't reply for a minute; he just studies me, thoughtful. "What about those girls, Jenny and what's-her-name, the goth one? I thought I saw them with balloons out there."

"Yup," I reply quietly. "It's Jenny's birthday too. We have the same."

Charlie is still waiting with an expectant look, so I take a breath, and find myself explaining to him. "We always used to celebrate together. Last year, we went down to Brighton for a gig, and then the year before, Jenny's mum treated us to makeovers, but now…" I let out a wistful sigh. "Now I get to watch her with her balloons, and presents, and friends, while I sit here with my pathetic loser cupcake. Alone." I stop, suddenly realizing how much I've shared with him, but Charlie doesn't look fazed at all.

"Moping much?" He snags another scoop of icing. "And you're not alone. I'm here."

"Until Lucy shows," I correct him. "Or are you done with her already?"

"Don't say it like that," Charlie protests. "We had a mutual parting of the ways." He breaks off a chunk of cake this time, and inhales it without even chewing. "Well, actually, she dumped me. Said I was a pig; can you believe that?" He grins, icing smeared across his chin.

"The mind boggles." I feel a sudden urge to wipe the sugar off his face. With my tongue. I look away, mortified.

"So what happened?" Charlie asks, oblivious to my face-licking impulses. "With your friends, I mean. Did you have a massive bitch fight? With pillows. In your underwear?"

I give him a withering stare.

He grins. "No, I mean it. What went down?"

I shrug, silent. The truth is, even I don't know. There was no fight, or reason why; she just started spending more time with Sascha, and less with me. I tried tagging along at first, to their after-school hang-outs down the park, and the skanky pub in Lingfield that never asked for ID, but it was clear I didn't belong.

Charlie must see something in my expression, because he gives me a sympathetic look. "People change." He nods, reaching for the cake.

I slap his hand back. "Save some for me!"

He sighs, breaking what's left into two pieces and handing me the bigger one with a martyrish look, like it's the biggest sacrifice ever. "I don't know why you even came in today. I always skive on my birthday. It's like a rule."

"I thought about it, but my mum—"

"But nothing." He pushes back his chair. "Let's go."

"Where?"

"I don't know. London, Brighton…" He grins. "Trains come every ten minutes. We'll figure it out after."

"No, but…" I blink. We. He said *we*. As in… "You mean, go. With you?"

"Why not? We've only got economics later. I didn't do the homework."

"You never do." I sit, but he's still there, waiting. "Is this some kind of joke, because I'm really not—"

"Jesus, Vita, stop thinking so hard." Charlie flicks my braids. "You don't want to be here; I really don't want to be here. So we make it so we're not here. Simple." Charlie beams, because to him it really is that simple. Never mind that I've never skived off in my life, let alone to just waltz on up to London with a boy who … who…

"I can't," I say, because I really can't. Why doesn't he see that? "Thanks, really; it's sweet of you to even offer, but I'm not that girl." I stop. "I mean, I don't—"

"Have fun?" Charlie finishes for me. "Do what you want?" He reaches to flick my hair again. I duck away.

"No!" I protest. "I have fun!"

But he's already backing away. "Limited time offer, Vita. Going, going..."

I don't move. Charlie's smile slowly fades. "Oh. Right. Should've known..." I watch, torn, as he pushes his hands back in his pockets and shrugs with trademark nonchalance. "Suit yourself."

He saunters away.

I'm surprised by the rush of disappointment I feel as he disappears from view. But that's just stupid. Of course I can't skip out on college for no good reason. And with Charlie Sutton! Doesn't he know I'm not one of his harem? I'm not delusional enough to think I'm special, that he'll change for me, that I'll get anything more from him than a half-hour of passionate kisses – his arms tight around me, my fingers tangled in his choppy dark hair...

Before I can take another second to think,

I grab my coat and bag and race out of the library after him.

"Charlie!"

He doesn't turn.

"Charlie, wait up!" I catch up with him in the foyer, yanking him to a stop. He finally turns, arching an eyebrow at me: the old, arrogant Charlie Sutton back in place.

"Yes," I say quickly. "I mean, let's go; get out of here. If you still want to?"

He pauses, and I become painfully aware of the people around us – of Jenny and Sascha on their spot on the stairs, surrounded by gift wrap and balloons.

"Well?" I gulp, trying to keep the tremor from my voice. If he blows me off here, in front of everyone...

"Sure thing, babe." Charlie's face relaxes into his familiar grin.

I exhale in relief. "Don't call me babe." I fall into step beside him as we head towards the exit. I can see the curious stares, hear the intake of breath as people turn to gossip, but I don't care. For the first time in months, I don't care what anyone might think of me. It doesn't matter.

"What nickname would you prefer?" Charlie asks, teasing. "Pumpkin? Poochie? Fluffikins?"

I glare. "You make me sound like a pet chihuahua."

"Fluffikins it is." He drapes an arm over my shoulder, casual as can be, but the warmth, the weight of it, makes my pulse kick up, dancing in my veins. "So where does my fluffikins want to go?"

"I don't know, sweetie-pie," I shoot back, breathless. "Anywhere. Nowhere."

"Helpful."

"I try."

He pushes the door open, and we step out into the grey, wet world. Rain drizzles down, cold under the collar of my coat, and for a moment, I'm tempted to just turn round – go and hide back in the library, in the warm safety of my secret carrel, with my books and homework and all the things I'm good at, the things I know for sure. Then Charlie turns back and holds out his hand, and all my second thoughts become irrelevant. Everything becomes irrelevant, save that thrill in my blood, and the shiver that has nothing to do with the crappy English weather.

With a couple of short steps, I close the distance between us and take his hand.

I want this, and I don't care why.

My

EMBARRASSING

Mother

Monica McInerney

Jack Kelly isn't my boyfriend. I wish he was. I have wished that for nearly five years.

Jack is like this: tall, thin, shy, smart. He's nearly sixteen.

I am like this: short, regular size, also shy, smartish. I'm nearly sixteen too.

Jack has a habit. He bites his nail. He has ten fingernails, but he only bites one of them. The one on the little finger of his right hand. He does it when he is nervous, or embarrassed.

My habit? I blush. Not sweetly, as though I am in *Pride and Prejudice*. I blush as though someone has injected red paint into my skin. I do it in class if I'm asked to speak; I do it if a shop assistant says,

"Can I help you?" Basically, I am pretty much red all of the time. I've learned to live with it. I wear my hair long to hide my face as much as possible. A perfect hairstyle for me would be Cousin Itt's. Mum says my blushing is delightful. Sweet. All the words you use to describe, I don't know, a dough- nut. I don't want to be like a doughnut. I'd like to be cool. Enigmatic. Aloof. With a mysterious past, like a French orphan. Not an actual orphan – I'd miss Mum too much – but something more inter- esting than my actual self. Mum tells me this is just a stage I'm going through.

Mum's thirty-six. Between us, I think that's *ancient*, but one of her favourite sayings is: "You're as young as you feel and I feel fantastic!" She not only thinks she's young, she also thinks she's cool. She completely ignores me when I try to tell her – really diplomatically – that the clothes she wears are, well, not quite right for someone her age. Jeans with studs on them. T-shirts covered in multi- coloured sequins that she has sewn on *herself*. "Oh, what's wrong with a bit of individuality, darling? We can't both go around looking gloomy, can we?" she says to me. I *don't* look gloomy. I'm not emo or a goth, either. I just like how I feel when I wear all black. It's like being in disguise. Or behind a shield.

Mum's always telling me she remembers her teenage years very clearly. She likes to talk to me about rites of passage and how one day none of my teenage torments will matter. She knows about peer groups and queen bees. But what she doesn't realize is that actually these things *do* matter. Maybe they *won't* matter in ten years' time, when my high school years are far behind me, but sadly, right now, high school *is* where I am and I can't just rise above it all.

Especially not when I get as embarrassed as I did today. I mean it. If it was possible to explode from too-rapid blood flow to the cheeks, I would have been lying dead on the school canteen floor.

And it's all Mum's fault. Mum and her clothes.

It's a long story. And to tell it properly, I need to give you some basic information about myself.

I live in a country town in south-eastern Australia. Mum and I moved here from Melbourne after she and my dad got divorced. I was six at the time. I still see Dad. But he's pretty busy in Sydney with his new wife and kids now. Mum is a busy person too. As soon as we moved to our town, she joined committees and volunteered for raffle-ticket selling. Before long we couldn't walk down the town's main street without lots of people saying, "Hi, Renee!" (Sorry, I should have said that earlier; that's her name, Renee. I'm Lily. As in the flower. Mum says it was because I looked a bit blue when I was born. Good thing I wasn't born yellow or I'd be Daffodil!)

Mum's also a really friendly and positive person. Too positive, sometimes. I read that book *Pollyanna* once, where the girl (Pollyanna) sees the bright side of everything (to a frankly alarming degree; I mean, she gets given crutches for Christmas one year and says she is GLAD because she DOESN'T need them!!). Mum's like that, always so enthusiastic and generous about people, which is an excellent personality trait, I know, but it does mean she gets taken advantage of sometimes. Even though she's a city person by birth, she's not that streetwise. I always think I see through people much easier and more quickly than she can.

Which brings me back to my main topic.

Jack. Or more specifically, Jack and his mother, Shona.

They moved to our town the year I turned ten. Shona was (still is) the same age as my mum. She hadn't married Jack's father so she wasn't a divorcee like Mum, but she and Jack's dad had split up and so she was a single mum too. If I was to describe Shona in one word, I'd pick "flighty". I read it in a book once and it suits Shona perfectly. She is like a flighty, colourful butterfly, flitting from person to person, subject to subject and, as my mum learned to her peril, man to man. But I'm jumping ahead of myself.

About a millisecond after they'd moved here, Mum was round at their house with a tray of cakes.

I can imagine her saying, "Welcome! You've got a son the same age as my daughter, fantastic! Come for dinner!"

So they did. That same night.

I can still remember the first time I saw Jack. I was used to boys, of course. My primary school was co-ed. I'd had pop star crushes too. But – and this is no exaggeration – I felt something special the first time I saw Jack. A kind of shimmer inside me. I know I was only ten and this is probably fanciful (another of my favourite f words), but I remember thinking, *You're going to be special to me*.

Mum and Shona got on instantly, like two houses on fire. I mean that, despite all the horrible things that happened later. All through that long summer holiday, they laughed and gossiped and swapped single-parent stories. They also swapped clothes. Seriously. One person with Mum's fashion sense was bad enough, but to have two of them roaming the town? That aside, it was good to see Mum so happy. Shona perked Mum up and Mum calmed Shona down. And while they became friends, so did Jack and me. I had other friends, but most of them had gone away to beach houses or relatives. That summer became my "Summer with Jack".

We spent hours together. I heard all about the different towns he'd lived in, and all about his grandmother, Shona's mother, who had lived with them. But a year ago she died, and they had to move out of her flat, and to our town, where rents are cheaper. Jack told me that he'd really loved his grandmother and he still really missed her. Most of the boys I knew would never admit liking let alone loving their grandmother, but not Jack. He said his grandmother was not only kind, but also really funny. He told me she'd grown up in Ireland and had loads of brilliant Irish sayings. Sometimes, when we were playing a board game, or hanging out at the pool, or doing any of the things we did that summer, out of the blue Jack would use one of her sayings.

"She'd shame the devil, that one," if he saw

one of the older girls prancing about in a bikini or skimpy shorts trying to get attention. Or if he saw a larger-sized girl, he'd say, "What a fine strong agricultural girl." Or if he was really hungry, he'd say, "I could eat a scabby child through the bars of a cot." It used to make me laugh and laugh. He didn't do it in an Irish accent either, just in his own Australian accent, which made it even funnier. We'd try and make up our own sayings. "I'm so hungry I could eat a three-legged horse." "I'm so hungry I could eat a flock of mice on toast."

Sometimes Mum's boyfriend, Pete (the town plumber), would come round too. He and Mum had met when he came to our house to do some work. He was divorced too. One thing (our blocked pipes) led to another (a drink with Mum in the local pub) and then another (dinner in the local pub). By the time Shona and Jack moved to our town, Mum and Pete-the-Plumber had been seeing each other for nearly a year. It was pretty serious. I think Mum had been about to ask him to move in with us. (She kept asking me how I would feel if he was around more often – a giveaway, really.) Which was why it was even more upsetting when Pete and Shona ran off together.

But I'm jumping ahead again.

That summer, Jack and I did mostly outside things – swimming, picnics. I barely picked up a book, which was unlike me. Usually I read two or three a week. Jack seemed happier being outside than inside reading. Which was why it wasn't until we went back to school that I made my discovery.

Jack couldn't read or write properly.

He was in my class (it was a small primary school) and I started to notice he could only answer some questions. Ones about numbers, yes. Words, no. At first I thought he was just shy. Then, one night after school, Jack came over to our house to do his homework. We did our maths homework first. All fine. Then science – drawing cells – also fine. Then English. That's when I saw it. His writing was *mad*! All back to front and none of the words made sense.

I thought he was joking at first. I said, "It looks

like a hen dipped in ink ran across the page." (I was actually trying to mimic his grandmother.) But he didn't smile. He reacted strangely. He started biting his nail. He wouldn't look at me. Then he got up and said he was going to get a drink. While he was gone, I picked up his English notebook and leafed through it. Every page was covered in his strange scribbling.

Some people say it's bad for kids to watch too much TV, but sometimes it has its positive sides. This was one of those occasions. The previous week, I'd seen a documentary on MTV about Tom Cruise, and part of it was about him being dyslexic. I'd never heard the word before then. (I actually thought at first that it meant very sporty, because in his films Tom Cruise is always running and jumping and leaping out of planes.) The TV show explained that it's a kind of learning disorder. They interviewed a dyslexia expert who said that people who had it just saw letters differently; it didn't mean the dyslexic children or adults were stupid, far from it – in fact, often they were very,

very bright. Leonardo da Vinci was dyslexic; so is Steven Spielberg. It's also treatable, the TV show said. People with it just have to be taught in different ways.

I told Mum about Jack's notebook and my suspicions. And Mum, being the world's most enthusiastic fixer of any tiny problem, went over to Shona's that same night to talk about it. Mum told me later that Shona got really defensive at first, but then she got weepy and eventually confessed that she had trouble reading and writing too. Long story short, Mum and Shona sat down for a long chat and it turned out Shona was dyslexic too, and her mother had been as well. One of the reasons they'd moved so much was that Jack was always getting into trouble at school, and of course he was, because he'd never had the right attention or extra tuition he needed. Shona had thought it just ran in the family and there was nothing they could do about it.

Mum was in heaven. A problem to solve! She got on to the school the next day. Within a week,

Jack was getting extra help. Within a couple of months, he got a bit more confident in class and even started reading his work aloud sometimes. When we did our homework together, I noticed his handwriting was bigger than mine, and he took longer, but his letters were nearly always the right way round now.

I was so proud of him. I never said anything to anyone else at school about the dyslexia – that was Jack's business – but I would always say, "Great story, Jack!" after he'd read it out loud during English class. One of my friends, Mandy (whose nickname is Mouth; you'll understand why soon), said to me once, "Why don't you marry Jack if you love him so much?" And I had all sorts of retorts ready but then I thought, *I would marry him, actually,* so I just blushed and said nothing – except, of course, the blush was my answer and Mandy knew it. She watched Jack and me like a hawk from then on.

Shona was so grateful. She kept going on and on about what a wonderful friend Mum was. It was all a bit over the top really. Now, of course, I get it; she was obviously covering up her guilt with all that gushing, because she was already having the affair with Pete. Jack, however, didn't make a big deal about the whole dyslexia thing. He and I just kept being friends as normal, after school, on weekends. Except one night he passed me a note, when we were at my house doing our homework. It said "Knaht uoy." It took me a second to realize it was a kind of dyslexic joke. *Thank you*, backwards.

"Any time, Jack," I said.

And I got that shimmer again, and I blushed. And there was a second, just a second, when I thought he was going to lean across and kiss me – only on the cheek or something – but Mum came in and it didn't happen, which was just as well because that would have made what happened next even worse.

What happened was Mum caught Shona and Pete together. (Not that I heard all the details at the time; back then she just told me that it was all over between her and Pete, and her and Shona. I was only ten then; I didn't need or want to hear about adults being caught in bed with each other when they were supposed to be seeing other people, i.e. my mum.)

For the next two weeks, Mum cried and cried. She told me she never wanted me to talk to Shona again, or to Jack. She said he must be cut from the same cloth, not to be trusted, two-timing, treacherous, lots of t words. I liked Jack so much, but I loved my mum even more. So I did what she told me. I stopped talking to Jack, stopped inviting him home after school, stopped looking at him, even though I missed him so much it actually hurt. I'd see him in the schoolyard, on his own a lot, reading – he seemed to be reading all the time now that had got sorted out – but I didn't talk to him. I couldn't. One day I saw him coming towards me, but I turned my back on him. I had to. For Mum's sake. He didn't come over again.

Mandy-the-Mouth noticed, of course. "He's thick, anyway," Mandy said, thinking she was being a friend, I guess. "You know he has to go to remedial reading classes, don't you?"

"He's not thick," I said, defending him before I knew what I was doing. I told her everything, because I wanted her to know the truth and also because it felt good talking about Jack, a way of keeping him close. Mandy listened, but then all she wanted to do was talk about Tom Cruise, so I didn't get to talk about Jack as much as I'd hoped.

Meanwhile, Shona was still trying to be friends with Mum, even though she was now with Pete. She kept turning up at our house but Mum wouldn't answer the door and nor did I.

"She's absolutely brazen," I heard one of Mum's friends say. They'd all flocked around her, each with an opinion of Shona. "Morals of an alley cat." "I never trusted her from the start."

Shona and Pete obviously got sick of the gossip pretty quickly, because within a month word got around that they were moving as soon as the school term finished. All three of them. I secretly hoped Jack would come and say goodbye before he left. He didn't. Then I thought he'd leave a note for me in the letter box instead. He didn't. I felt really sad about it, but there was nothing I could do. His mum must have banned him from me just like my mum had banned me from him.

Fast-forward five years, to exactly three months ago, when Mum came home with the news. "Guess who's back in town!"

You guessed it. Shona. Without Pete. It turned out that Pete had run off with someone new. And yes, Mum's source had told her, Jack was back too; and yes, he would be going to school. Into year eleven at the high school, like me.

I asked Mum outright. "Am I still banned from speaking to him?"

"You were never banned from talking to him. It was Shona who did the dirty on us, not Jack."

"But you told me never to talk to him again."

"Lily! I'd never have done that. I knew what good friends you and Jack were."

That's called "selective memory". I've read about it. But what was the point in making a fuss about it now? What would it change?

The first day of the new school term came around. Our high school was big, with more than five hundred kids in it. Yet I saw Jack within minutes of arriving. He was sitting on his own, in the quadrangle. Reading. If I'd got a shimmery feeling when I first saw him as a ten-year-old, it was now a starburst feeling. I was nearly sixteen now, after all. A woman, not a kid. I'd even had my first boyfriend. It only lasted a month (my decision – he was nice, just not really my type). But I'd been glad to get my first kiss out of the way. I liked kissing very much. I was very interested in doing more of it. Just not with that boy.

Even though Jack was sitting down, I could see that he had grown tall. But he was still skinny. He still had really black hair that stuck up at the back. And he still bit his nail when he was nervous. I noticed him do it as we lined up for morning assembly. I noticed him do it as we waited outside our different homerooms. I couldn't stop noticing him. I wanted to say something to him, but even thinking about it made me glow red. I didn't know how to approach him, what to say. And if he wanted to talk to me, he could make the first move, couldn't he? But he didn't seem to see me. Or so I thought.

Three days later, I was sitting outside at lunchtime with a group of my classmates when he came across the yard towards us. Mandy was sitting beside me. She still had a big mouth. She also had a good memory. Too good.

As Jack walked closer, there was a second, just a second, when he and I were looking right at each other, right into each other's eyes. As if we were the only two people in the schoolyard. As if those five years hadn't passed. As if we were ten again, not nearly sixteen. As if what had happened hadn't happened. I knew the look in his eyes. It was a kind look, a sweet look, an "I hope we can be friends again" look. I knew, because I was feeling the exact same things.

But Mandy didn't know that. She saw him looking at me and saw me looking at him, and she saw me blush, and she told me afterwards that she thought it was because I was still angry about his mum running off with my mum's boyfriend. But it wasn't. My blush was just a proper old-fashioned "oh God look how gorgeous Jack is now and here he comes to talk to me" blush.

He was nearly within speaking distance and was still looking at me, when Mandy piped up, at top voice beside me. "Come for another reading and writing lesson, Jack, have you?"

She meant well, she told me a zillion times after. "I was just trying to protect you."

But Jack didn't know that. He obviously thought – and why wouldn't he? – that I'd told everyone about his dyslexia in a mean way and that we were taunting him. He stopped in front of us, in front of me, as if he was frozen. And he looked at me again, looked really long and hard at me, as if I had disappointed him in a way he'd never thought possible. And then he walked away. Without saying a word.

I wanted to cry. I wanted to ring Mum and ask her to come and get me. All those things that kids do but I couldn't do any more because I was nearly sixteen and the last thing I wanted to do was draw any more attention to myself. Or to Jack.

A week went past. Another week. I saw him in the schoolyard every day. He was either on his own or with a group of guys. Not the cool group, the brainy-but-a-bit-odd group. He never looked back at me. I tried sending him ESP messages. They didn't work.

One night, Mum told me she'd seen Shona in the street. I hadn't told her about me and Jack. She didn't know I was crying myself to sleep about him. I tried to sound breezy. "Did you throw rocks at her? Try and run her over?"

She frowned. "Why would I do that?"

I rolled my eyes. "Uh, Mum, remember Shona? The one who stole your boyfriend?"

"That was years ago. She actually did me a favour. If Pete ran off so easily he wasn't a good man anyway."

See what I mean? My mum makes Pollyanna look evil.

I tried to put Jack out of my mind. I tried to

get used to the sad, stone-like feeling in my chest. I studied. I played netball. I tried not to notice him at school and in town. I tried to forget the look of disappointment he'd given me. Mandy kept apologizing. I told her I was fine. She knew I was lying.

Then came Mum's turn to volunteer in the school canteen. "Please, Mum, whatever you do," I begged the night before, "please don't wear anything that would embarrass me."

I shouldn't have said it. I should have stayed quiet, and I should have stayed home that night. But I was staying at my friend Nicola's house, so we could watch a DVD of *Jane Eyre* in preparation for our English class. If I'd been home, I would have noticed a gleam in Mum's eye, seen her stand in front of her wardrobe, and heard her say out loud, "Lily cares far too much what other people think of her; it's time to shock her out of it."

I would have somehow stopped her reaching for that rainbow-coloured ripped T-shirt and the polka dot miniskirt. Stopped her reaching for the hair gel and eyeliner. Stopped her leaning down and taking out the blue Doc Martens.

But I hadn't been there.

Which meant I walked into the canteen at lunchtime today to see my mother standing behind the counter, looking like a deranged escapee from a 1980s punk music video. In front of *everyone*.

"Oh my God, Lily! You're completely bright red!" It was Mandy, coming up beside me.

I said nothing, just stared down at my feet. I bet they were bright red inside my shoes too. I fought back sudden tears. I didn't dare look up. This was a nightmare. The canteen is always so crowded at lunchtime. Everyone would see her. My friends and classmates. My teachers. Even people I didn't know would see her and tease me.

"I can't decide who looks worse," Mandy said, too loudly. "Have they done it for a dare?"

They? There was someone else in embarrassing clothes? I peered through my hair.

Mandy was right. There was a second woman behind the canteen counter. She was wearing a gold shimmery top so skintight I was amazed she could breathe. Tight blue pants that looked like they'd been sprayed on. Her hair was backcombed into a kind of a beehive. She looked like Olivia Newton-John in the final scene of *Grease*. She made my mother look like Audrey Hepburn.

It was Shona. Jack's mother, Shona.

I didn't see him come up behind me. I didn't know he was there until I heard his voice, right behind me. "She'd shame the devil, that one," he said.

I spun round. He didn't look embarrassed. He didn't seem mortified. His expression was calm. Then he bit the nail of his little finger and I knew he was nervous.

I swallowed. I wanted to say a thousand things. *I've missed you, Jack. I'm sorry you left the way you did all those years ago. I'm sorry Mandy said what she said. I'd never have teased you about your dyslexia.* But I said nothing. All I could do was stare at him and go even more bright red.

He didn't seem to notice. He didn't seem to care that the kids around us were giggling about our mothers, either. He just stood beside me as if I'd been holding a place for him in the queue.

"Thank God it's lunchtime," he said, after another moment's silence.

I could only nod.

"I'm so hungry I could eat a scabby child," he said.

I stared at him. I found my voice. "Through the bars of a cot?" I said.

"Through the bars of a cot," he said.

Another second passed.

"Want to go halves?" he said.

"Yes please," I said.

He smiled at me. I smiled back.

We walked up to the counter together.

Postscript

I always hate it when stories finish like that, so here's what happened next. My mum served him; his mum served me. My mum was really friendly to him; his mum was actually a bit over-the-top friendly to me.

We found out later that his mum had called round to my mum's the night before to plead forgiveness and make friends again. Mum had been choosing her embarrassing canteen-duty outfit. She said she didn't think she would go through with it. But then Shona said she could volunteer and dress up too, wouldn't that be a lark? The more they talked, and the more wine they drank, the more hilarious the idea seemed.

"Sorry if we embarrassed you," they both said. But anyone could see they weren't sorry. They were laughing too much.

In hindsight, I'm not sorry either. Because if they hadn't both turned up at school looking like that, I don't know when or if Jack and I would have started talking again.

Or started meeting up after school again.

Or started seeing each other on weekends.

Or talked about all that had happened to us in the five years since we'd seen each other.

Or said sorry to each other for not staying friends back then.

Or told each other how much we had missed each other.

Or kissed each other for the first time.

But they did. And we did.

And that kiss with Jack was the best kiss I'd ever had in my whole life.

Until he kissed me a second time.

Lost
in
Translation

Sinéad Moriarty

When you're sixteen and a half, not particularly good-looking and have three mean sisters and a best friend with boobs like Jordan's, you take any compliments you can. In fact, you eat them up.

My mother tells me I'm "interesting-looking" – which is actually worse than being called ugly. My sisters don't sugar-coat it for me. They tell me all the time that I'm ugly, all except for my younger sister, Annie, who says I look like the actress Amy Adams, only my eyes are smaller. Have you seen Amy Adams's eyes?! They're tiny! So I have *raisin* eyes and brownish-red hair – like those red setter dogs, as my sister Joan constantly reminds me.

(Sometimes when she's feeling particularly bitchy, which is most of the time, she woofs at me.)

So when a gorgeous Spanish guy told me that my tiny raisin eyes were like pools of emeralds sparkling in the moonlight, I chose to believe him – and that's when things got complicated...

Mum cried at the airport. It was so embarrassing. She howled into my shoulder! I could see people looking around to see where the werewolf was.

"Mum, seriously, stop," I hissed. "I'm going to Spain for two weeks, not Australia for ten years."

Mum fished around in her handbag for a tissue. She pulled out two blue Bic pens, one of which had no cap and was leaking, a half-eaten granola bar, a huge set of keys that a prison warden would have been proud of, a packet of Silvermints, a book on how to be successful in every aspect of your life and, finally, a raggedy old tissue. She blew her nose.

"I know it's only two weeks, but it's the first time you've gone away on your own and I'm just worried." She sniffed.

I sighed and for the millionth time reminded her that I wasn't going away on my own. I was going with my best friend, Chloe White, and her parents.

Mum looked over at Mr and Mrs White. Gerry White was talking furiously into his mobile phone. We could hear him shouting, "Not bloody good enough. We're not settling for less than two million." Norma White was sitting, drinking a coffee with her sunglasses on, even though it was raining outside.

"I won't get a wink of sleep until you come back," Mum said.

Well, I knew *that* was a big fat lie. Mum sleeps like the dead. The minute her head hits the pillow she is gone to the Land of Nod and nothing can wake her up. Even when Dad left and everyone else was up all night crying, Mum was snoring in her bedroom. She says it's the only time she gets to switch off. If sleep were an Olympic sport, she would be a gold-medal winner.

Chloe came over to Mum and me then. She was wearing a gorgeous Marc Jacobs minidress and Miu Miu wedges. I looked down at my Primark maxi dress and felt very uncool. Chloe always has the best clothes. Her mum takes her shopping once a month and buys her all designer stuff. My mum takes me shopping once a year and buys me school shoes and trainers.

"Hi, Mrs Jones." Chloe smiled at my mother. To me she said, "Look, Jenny, we need to go through security now. Are you ready?"

I'd never been more ready. I was going on a two-week holiday to Spain with my best friend and her very rich parents. We were staying in a five-star hotel on the beach. I would be away from my three sisters for fourteen blissful days. I couldn't wait.

I pulled away from Mum's clinging hands. "Goodbye, Mum. You need to go or you'll be late for work," I reminded her.

"Call me when you land," she told me. "Call me every day. If you don't call, I'll be worried."

"OK, OK, I will. Please, Mum, I need to go now."

I pecked her on the cheek, turned round and walked through the departure gate.

Spain, here I come!

When we landed and the aeroplane doors had opened, the warm summer air wrapped around me like a cosy blanket. It was great to feel heat on my bones. It was the fifteenth of July, and so far in Dublin this year our summer had consisted of rain (lots of), hailstones and even sleet on one very special day. I was thrilled to be in sunny Spain.

Mrs White seemed to be in better form when we landed too. By then she had knocked back three of those little bottles of wine. She had started smiling after the second bottle and, although she hadn't taken her dark glasses off, had told us we could order whatever we wanted from the in-flight menu. Chloe had ordered everything, taken tiny bites of it all and then said she was full. So I'd ended up eating most of it – sandwiches, crisps, chocolate bars and crackers and cheese. It was fantastic!

When we arrived at the hotel, my jaw nearly hit the floor. It was incredible. You walked through the huge white-marble lobby, out of some French doors and you were on a white sandy beach. There were about a hundred sunloungers in neat lines, each with a soft squishy blue and white striped cushion to lie on. Each chair even had its own parasol. There were waiters in crisp white T-shirts and navy shorts scurrying around delivering drinks and snacks to the sunbathers.

"Let's get our togs on," Chloe suggested, and we ran upstairs to our big bedroom to change.

We were back down in ten minutes. Me in my H&M red and white polka dot bikini and Chloe in her Missoni swimsuit with a plunging neckline. Although she is only sixteen, Chloe has really big boobs – I think they are even bigger than Kim Kardashian's! I am jealous of them. Mine are like two fried eggs, sunny side up. I have a boy's shape – tall, long and lean. Chloe has a womanly shape – small, with big boobs, a small waist and big hips. She wants to be thinner and I want to be curvier.

We lay on our sunloungers and applied sun-cream to each other's backs.

"I think I've died and gone to heaven," I said, looking around at the beautiful beach and the deep blue sea.

Chloe shrugged. "It's OK, I guess. I'm usual-ly here on my own with Mum and Dad, which is *sooooo* boring. Dad spends his whole time on the phone and Mum just shops and drinks wine. I'm so glad they let me bring a friend this year. It's going to be so much more fun with you here."

"I'm very happy to oblige." I grinned. "Last summer we went to Kerry for a week. We stayed in a two-bedroom mobile home that Mum's boss lent us. It rained every single day, but Mum insist-ed on going to the beach for picnics in between the showers. We sat on the cold wet sand, eating sand-wiches, shivering, moaning and fighting. At night the only thing to do was play cards or Scrabble. Can you imagine four girls, ranging in ages from fourteen to twenty, stuck in a small mobile home for a week? It was hell."

Chloe smiled. "I dunno. It sounds kind of fun. At least you have people to play with, or fight with or whatever. Being an only child sucks. I'd love to have three sisters."

I snorted. "No, you wouldn't. Trust me, it's no fun."

"My mum really wanted more kids. She had loads of miscarriages after I was born and eventually just gave up trying. Sometimes when she drinks too much wine she gets upset about it. It's mortifying. I hate it when she gets all teary. Dad can't cope with her when she's like that either. He just gets furious and tells her to be grateful for all the things she does have. She says material things mean nothing to her and don't make up for lost babies. But Dad says her credit card bills suggest the opposite – and they end up having a massive argument."

"At least your dad is around to argue with her. Mine's MIA."

"Does he never get in touch with any of you?" Chloe asked.

I shook my head. "No, none of us. He lives in

England now with his new woman and doesn't give a damn about us."

"I'm never getting married," Chloe announced.

"Me neither. Unless Justin Timberlake asks me."

"Or Robert Pattinson."

"Or Taylor Lautner."

We giggled.

"I'm hungry; let's order some food," Chloe suggested. "What do you fancy?" She looked up from the menu. "Speaking of something I fancy ... he's cute!"

A tall boy with pale skin and brown curly hair was walking by. He had nice blue eyes and a good body, but he wasn't really my type. He looked too Irish. I only wanted to meet dark, handsome Spanish boys on this holiday.

"I recognize him," Chloe said. "He's in school with my cousin. I'm pretty sure he's the captain of the rugby team. I bags him!"

I laughed. "You're welcome to him."

Chloe followed him with her eyes. "Dylan. That's his name. I'll have to think of a way to get chatting to him later." Chloe's stomach rumbled. "What are you having to eat?"

Mum had told me to always order the cheapest thing on the menu and only ever ask for tap water because it was free. She said people didn't like guests who were always asking for things. It was important to be an excellent guest. I scanned the menu. The cheapest thing was a side salad.

"I'll just have a green salad," I said.

Chloe looked at me. "Are you sure?"

I nodded.

She sighed. "No wonder you're so thin. I'll have the burger and fries."

I was delighted. I knew Chloe would only have one bite of the burger and a couple of fries. I'd be able to eat the rest.

The waiter came over to take our order. He was my height, really tanned and had jet-black hair and big brown eyes. He looked about eighteen. His T-shirt was very fitted and showed off his muscles. He was *so* my type.

"*Buenas tardes*. My name is Carlos. How can

I help you today?" he asked.

"I'm Jenny. Jennifer," I said.

Chloe waved the menu at him. "We'd like a burger, fries and a side salad and two Cokes."

"Please," I added. "I mean, *por favor.*"

Carlos winked at me. "I'll bring it right away," he said in a beautiful Spanish accent. He rolled his r's. It was very sexy.

I blushed; he was so hot.

Fifteen minutes later, Carlos was back with our food. His fingers brushed my hand when he passed me my Coke. I shuddered. It was like an electric volt down my arm. I looked up at him and his eyes locked with mine. Wow, he really was gorgeous.

"Bon appétit," he said, grinning at me as he walked off.

Chloe smirked. "So is Carlos more your type than Dylan?"

"What?" I blushed.

"Oh my God, it's so obvious – you're practically drooling."

I busied myself with my salad. "No, I'm not."

Chloe popped a chip into her mouth. "Come on, admit it – you fancy him. I can see why – he is cute. But there are loads of hot Spanish guys here. Don't fall for the first one you meet. Besides, I thought he was a bit too smooth."

I disagreed but said nothing. My hand was still tingling from his touch.

At dinner that night, I ordered gazpacho and chicken, the least expensive starter and main course on the dining-room menu. I thought the gazpacho was going to be some kind of Spanish cheese, but it actually turned out to be cold vegetable soup. It was gross! Chloe and her mum and dad all had *gambas* – which it turned out was a worse choice.

First of all Norma left the table to be sick, followed shortly by her husband. Chloe wasn't long after her parents – which left me at the table on my own. I didn't know what to do. Should I stay and wait to see if they came back or go back to our room and check on Chloe?

Just as I was getting up to go, Chloe's dad came in, looking green.

"I'm afraid we all seem to have food poisoning," he said. "Please go ahead and order dessert and anything else you fancy. Chloe's upstairs in bed. I'm sorry about all this. I'm disgusted with the hotel for serving bad—" Before he could finish his sentence, he had to rush off and be sick again.

Carlos, the waiter from the beach, appeared in front of me like a vision. "Good evening, señorita, how are you?"

"Oh, hi," I said, trying not to blush, and thrilled to see him.

"I am sorry to hear your friends are all sick. It's very bad luck."

"Yes, it is, really awful."

"Would you like to order a dessert?"

I hesitated. I knew Mum would have said not to, especially with the others sick, but I had seen the most amazing chocolate tart on the menu, and I really wanted to try it.

Carlos winked at me. "Go on, señorita, you are on holidays, no? Have a dessert – the chocolate one is fantastic." He kissed his fingers to demonstrate how delicious it was. "I will ask the chef to give a very big portion to my special friend."

How could I refuse that offer? So I ignored my mother's voice in my head telling me not to and ordered the chocolate dessert.

Carlos came back with a very large slice of tart and a scoop of cappuccino ice cream on the side. I picked up my spoon and tasted it. It was amazing.

"Wow!" I exclaimed.

Carlos grinned. "I tell you it's *fabuloso*."

"It really is," I said, shovelling another spoonful into my mouth.

"Carlos know this will make you happy." He smiled.

I wanted to smile back, but I knew I had chocolate all over my teeth so I just nodded enthusiastically.

"I made this myself," he announced.

"Really?" I was impressed.

"Yes, I am learning to be a pastry chef."

"Wow, that's brilliant. Well, this is incredible. Well done."

He beamed at me. *"Gracias."* Then he leaned over and whispered in my ear, "I am finishing the work in ten minutes. Do you want to go for a walk with me on the beach? Look at beautiful moon?"

I almost choked on my dessert. Was he really suggesting a moonlight walk? Just the two of us? My mother's voice popped right back into my head. "Never go off with strange men. No good will come of it. All men want is sex, especially Spanish men. They're all sex-mad over there. Sex and bull-fighting, that's all they're interested in. Stay away from them. Stay away from all boys until you've finished school."

I looked up at Carlos. He didn't look sex-mad. He didn't look like he spent all his time watching bullfights and seducing girls. He looked nice and normal and friendly and kind. I hesitated...

Sensing my uncertainty, Carlos added, "We will be like two friends, just walking and talking."

What the hell!

"OK, that sounds nice," I said.

"I meet you outside in ten minutes." He walked away and I admired his bum as he went.

I couldn't believe it! A gorgeous Spanish man who made incredible chocolate desserts had asked me out. This was the best holiday ever!

We sat side by side on the beach, very close but not actually touching, and stared up at the star-filled sky. Carlos pointed out the stars and constellations to me. He got most of them wrong, but I didn't want to contradict him. I liked listening to his deep voice, and so what if stargazing wasn't his strong point? He had a gorgeous face and a body to die for.

I asked him about his cooking.

"I want to be the best pastry chef in the world," he said. "I am going to study in France. I just need to save the money to go and then I will show the world what I can really do."

"Good for you. My mum says it's important to

have goals. I bet you'll be amazing – that chocolate dessert was unbelievable."

He took my hand and stared into my eyes. I tried to open them as wide as possible, so he wouldn't think they were tiny little crappy eyes.

"Thank you, Jennifer. You are a lovely girl with a big heart. Your eyes are like the green jewel – how you say it?"

"Emeralds?" I almost shouted.

"Yes, this is it – your eyes are like emeralds sparkling in the night. So beautiful."

I blushed from my toes to the top of my head. I was thrilled to pieces. No one had ever used the word "beautiful" to describe anything about me. "Do you really think so? You're not just saying it to be nice?"

He looked offended. "No! I only say things I am meaning. I am not a boy who says lies."

"Oh, OK, sorry. It's just that I never thought my eyes were anything to look at, and as for the rest of me – well, I'm just so plain and no boy has ever—"

I never got any further because Carlos leaned

over and kissed me, mid-conversation. Softly at first, just on the lips, and then he put his hands up and cupped my face and began to increase the pressure slightly. Slowly and gently he opened his mouth and kissed me deeply, wonderfully, amazingly, divinely, incredibly... I did not want it to stop EVER.

My body turned to jelly, and I leaned into the kiss and allowed the sensation of it to sink down to my toes. Irish boys did not kiss like this. My previous experiences of kissing had involved a lot of excess saliva, and whirling, twirling tongues that went so fast I couldn't keep up. Some tongues went clockwise and some went anticlockwise. And I had certainly never had my face cupped. I felt as if I were falling into space. This was kissing on a whole new level! Carlos had to be the Spanish champion kisser. He was incredible. And he didn't grab my boobs or try to put his hand up my skirt. He just kept kissing and stroking my cheek and then running his hands through my hair.

When he finally stopped – when we finally

came up for air – my head was spinning. He pulled back and smiled at me.

"You are very beautiful girl to kiss. You have the sweet lips."

"Right back at you," I said, catching my breath. I wanted to pinch myself. Was I dreaming? Things like this *never* happened to me.

"I have very much enjoy spending time with you."

"Me too," I gushed.

"We have good conversation, no?"

"Yes, we did," I answered enthusiastically. I didn't remember much conversation at all, but then again, I think my brain had stopped working after the kiss.

He looked at his watch and winced. "Ah, *lo siento*, I must go. I am working the breakfast tomorrow. I see you there? Yes?"

"Yes, definitely, yes, I'll be there. I'll be up early for breakfast. I will be the first there. I wouldn't miss it for anything."

He smiled. "I hope your family is feeling better

soon. OK, *muy bien*. Maybe tomorrow when I am finished my work we can be together again."

I stifled the sob rising in my throat. This drop-dead gorgeous guy wanted to be with me. Me?! Jenny of the fried-egg boobs and reddish-brown hair and raisin eyes.

I managed to whisper, "That would be lovely," before he turned to go and I began to cry with joy.

Viva España!

The next morning I sprang out of bed at seven. Chloe was still feeling awful from the food poisoning, but I asked her if she wanted any breakfast.

"Urgh, are you trying to make me vomit again? I couldn't look at food. I'm sorry, Jenny, but I can't even lift my head off the pillow. I'll try to get up later. Enjoy the beach. I'll text you when I'm up."

I was secretly delighted. Now I could sneak off with Carlos without having to explain anything to Chloe. I put on my nicest dress – it was a red and white striped sundress with a halter neck and a very low back. My fake tan was still unstreaked so the dress looked good on me. I put on tons of mascara and some lipgloss. I was going to add some liquid eyeliner but decided it might look a bit too much for nine o'clock in the morning. I strapped on my really high white wedge sandals and tottered down to breakfast.

Carlos was on the terrace, serving breakfast to a large family of Germans. He winked at me when I walked by. My heart soared. He looked even hotter than I remembered. Unfortunately I was put at a table in a different section, so he didn't serve me. But I spent all of my time watching him from behind my sunglasses. I barely ate any of my croissant or fruit. I was too nervous.

At ten thirty, Carlos strolled over to my table. "*Hola,* señorita!" He grinned at me. "You look lovely today. I have surprise for you. Meet me in half hour at the little cafe outside the hotel. The Siesta Cafe."

With that, he swung back round and went off to clear some tables. I rushed to the bathroom and re-applied some lipgloss. My phone rang. It was Mum.

I knew if I didn't answer, she'd just keep calling.

"Hi, Mum."

"Morning. How are you? Is everything all right? Are you having a nice time? Are you behaving? Were you out last night? What time were you in bed? I hope you haven't had any alcohol. Stay away from sangria. It looks like punch, but it's very potent. Are you being polite? Did you order the cheapest—"

I interrupted her. "Mum! I'm fine. I was in bed early. I haven't had any alcohol. Everything is fine. Seriously, stop fussing."

"I just worry about you," she said in a hurt voice.

I forced myself to be calm. "I know, Mum. But there is nothing to worry about. Everything is cool here. Look, I have to go."

"All right, all right. I'll leave you to it. Mind yourself, pet. I miss you."

"I will. Bye, Mum." I hung up and put my phone on silent. I didn't want any interruptions on my date.

♥ ♥ ♥

Carlos was waiting for me outside the cafe. He had changed out of his uniform into a pair of jeans and a blue T-shirt that showed off his lovely brown arms.

I suddenly felt awkward. "Hi." I smiled brightly to hide my shyness.

"Jenny, I am taking you to see the real Spain. Not this tourist place," Carlos told me as he gently took my hand and walked me over to a battered-looking yellow bus. We hopped on. Carlos paid for two tickets and then led me a window seat.

"Where are we going?" I asked.

"To an incredible restaurant. I want you to experience real Spanish cuisine. Not the burger and chips from the hotel. And the cakes and the pastries are unbelievable. The guy who makes them is the best in Spain."

"Wow, it sounds great. But I bet he's not as good as you."

Carlos grinned at me and put his arm round my shoulder. I snuggled into him as the bus took us away from the tourist cafes, restaurants and hotels. Up we climbed, into the hills behind Marbella. We passed through narrow streets with whitewashed houses. We waved at old ladies dressed in black, sitting on wicker chairs in the shade outside their front doors, sewing and knitting or fanning themselves in the heat. It was fantastic. I loved every second of it. I had never felt so free or so happy. This was about as far removed from my life in a convent school in rainy Dublin as possible. If Sister Katherine could see me now... I giggled to myself.

We eventually pulled up outside a restaurant called La Bodega in a small village square. It looked fancy. Carlos helped me down from the bus and held my hand as we walked into the restaurant. It was quite full: lots of very well-dressed people drinking wine and eating and chattering in Spanish, English, German and French. Carlos spoke to the manager, and we were given a lovely table in the corner. When I opened my menu, I was shocked to see how expensive it was.

Carlos leaned over and whispered, "This restaurant is very famous. Only very cool people know about it. You see over there – it is very famous Spanish movie star. I am wanting to comes here for a very long time, but I am waiting to meet the special girl." He stared into my eyes, and I swear my heart stopped beating.

As everything was so expensive and I didn't want Carlos to spend three weeks' wages on one lunch, I ordered the cheapest thing on the menu, which was risotto. Carlos ordered lobster and a bottle of champagne. I winced when I saw how much the champagne cost – one hundred euros for the bottle!

The food was gorgeous and the champagne was cold, bubbly and delicious. Carlos drank most of it, but the glass I had was lovely. During the meal, Carlos spent a lot of time talking about the food we were being served. I loved listening to his gorgeous accent as he told me about the best way to cook lobster, and that red wine should always be served at room temperature. He talked about the cooking academy he was going to study at in France – Le Cordon Bleu International in Paris. His eyes lit up when he described the training programme there. I was amazed at how much he knew about food and wine. None of the guys I knew in Ireland would dream of taking a girl to a beautiful restaurant. You'd be lucky if you got a cheeseburger and a milkshake in McDonald's.

In between the many courses – I think there were six in total – Carlos stroked my hand gently and stared into my eyes as he talked. I loved the feeling of being with someone who was so much more grown up than the immature boys I knew back home.

After a few wonderful hours, Carlos ordered the bill. When it came, he fished around in his jacket for money. "Oh, *mierda*!" he cursed. "I am forgetting my money at home. Oh no!"

"Oh God, um … OK … well, I have some money here," I said, scrambling about in my bag. I pulled out my purse.

Carlos handed me the bill. It was one hundred

and eighty euros. I felt sick. All I had in my wallet was sixty euros.

Carlos frowned as I fumbled with my notes. "Where is your credit card?" he asked.

"I don't have one."

"What?" He looked furious. "Everybody have the credit cards."

"Well, I don't. This is all the money I have." I was taken aback – why was he so cross?

He glared at me. "But you are staying in big hotel. You must have the credit card. I see your rich daddy."

I shook my head. "He's not my father. I'm just staying with my friend Chloe."

Carlos gritted his teeth. "You have no money and no credit card?"

I nodded.

"Your daddy is not rich?"

"My daddy buggered off to England nine years ago." I was beginning to get annoyed. My dream date was fast becoming a nightmare.

Carlos covered his face with his hands and

groaned. "How we are paying for this?" He waved the bill in my face. "I am thinking you are rich girl."

As the awful realization that Carlos had charmed me because he thought I was rich sank in, my blood began to boil. "Well, you backed the wrong horse. I'm not rich at all. And I presumed, seeing as it was your idea to come to this fancy restaurant, that *you* were going to pay."

"I am a waiter. I am not having money for this place!"

The manager came over then and spoke to Carlos. They had a heated discussion, which got progressively louder. Soon everyone in the restaurant was looking at us. Carlos kept pointing at me and shouting in Spanish. My face was bright red with shame and humiliation. What a fool I was, thinking a guy like him would ever fancy a girl like me!

After ten more minutes of watching Carlos's and the manager's arm-waving, chest-thumping, finger-pointing and head-shaking, I felt a tap on my shoulder.

"Are you all right?" a voice asked me in an Irish accent.

I spun round and found myself face to face with the guy Chloe had seen on the beach, the rugby player Dylan. I almost cried with happiness. The words tumbled out as I explained about Carlos being kind of my boyfriend and taking me here and thinking I was rich, and me not being rich at all because my poor mum was trying to support four daughters on her own, and how my friends had all been food poisoned in the fancy hotel, and how now I knew Carlos didn't like me for my emerald eyes and soft lips but because he thought I had a big bank account ... and then I actually started crying.

Dylan handed me a napkin to wipe my eyes and told me not to worry. He began to talk to the manager in perfect Spanish. Then he took out his wallet and *paid* the bill. Everyone stopped shouting. The manager went away and it was just me, Carlos and Dylan, my knight in shining armour.

Dylan, who was much taller and broader, said

something to Carlos in Spanish in a very low, steady voice. Carlos went red and then white. Then he nodded at Dylan and turned to me. "I am very sorry, Jenny. I make big mistake." And with that my phoney almost-boyfriend scurried out of the door.

I wanted to die. I wanted the floor to open up and swallow me. I had never been so mortified in my life. What kind of a fool was I?

Dylan offered to drive me back to my hotel. As I had no idea where I was and no clue how to get back, I accepted gratefully.

"How come you're here?" I asked him.

"I give the owner's son English lessons," he said. "My parents have a house here in this village and they're friends with the owners. I was finishing up the lesson and I heard all this shouting, so I stuck my head in to see what was going on."

"Thank God you did." I began to cry again.

"The guy's a jerk," Dylan said.

"And I'm a complete idiot."

"Don't blame yourself. These guys can be very manipulative."

I looked out of the window and sighed. "My sister Joan would say I told you so. She said Spanish waiters are a slippery lot. I feel like such a fool. Imagine believing a guy that gorgeous actually fancied me! Duh! How stupid can I be? Joan is right. I do look like a red setter."

Dylan roared out laughing. "Did your sister really say that?"

"Sometimes she woofs at me."

"No wonder your self-esteem is so low."

"She's not all bad. She works two jobs to help pay for me and my younger sister to go to private school. Mum can't afford it."

"Well, maybe all the hard work is affecting her eyesight."

I frowned. "What do you mean?"

"You look like Nicole Kidman."

I snorted. "Nice try, but I know you're just saying that because you feel sorry for me."

"I don't say things I don't mean."

"Seriously? For real? You're not just saying that because you witnessed me being publicly humiliated in a fancy restaurant?"

He shook his head. "You're a dead ringer for Nicole Kidman. Same hair, same mouth, same body."

I began to smile. Maybe this holiday wouldn't be so bad after all. I now knew that slobbery, dribbly, cold, wet kisses were not something I had to put up with for life. I now knew that a kiss could make your stomach flip, your legs go weak and your heart flutter. And for that, Carlos, I have to say *muchas gracias*!

And despite the public humiliation, Dylan had come to save me and he thought I looked like Nicole Kidman! Now all I had to do was explain to my best friend, Chloe, that I fancied Dylan too...

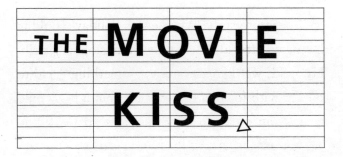

Joanna Nadin

It was a movie kiss.

It was Leonardo diCaprio and Claire Danes in armour and angel wings on the balcony in *Romeo and Juliet*. It was Burt Lancaster and Deborah Kerr on a black and white beach from here to eternity. It was Rhett and Scarlett, Holly Golightly and Paul, Jack and Rose.

It was me and him on the front step, on a rainy night in Nowheretown.

But that's what made it perfect.

I'd been kissed before. No less than three times by the age of seventeen. A near low in the history of high school, where success is measured in bases and popularity hangs on your choice of lipgloss.

My kisses were, in no particular order:

1. Jake Westville.

My ill-fated target in spin the bottle at Julie Newbery's twelfth birthday party. I ended up getting sick on chocolate fudge sundae; he ended up getting off with Julie. They are still together. Jake and Julie. I like to think my lack of prowess in the lip department somehow contributed to this alliterative union.

2. Ant McReady.

Film buff, Smiths devotee and year twelve's most committed emo. But it turned out his *Brokeback Mountain* obsession wasn't all about the horses or the sweeping scenery shots.

3. Luke Wright-Watson.

Behind McDonald's on the main street. Cheap cider blocked most of the two minutes twenty-seven seconds of this hell from memory. The rest I strive to do myself on a daily basis.

None of them made the earth move, the world stop, my toes tingle inside my black Chuck Taylors. None of them would make a cheap cable drama, let alone the Oscars.

Olly, my best friend, said I was suffering from film fatigue. That I'd overdosed on John Hughes high school high dramas, and as a result nothing on this side of the silver screen was ever going to come close. That I'd go to my grave never having had the perfect kiss if I measured it by Andie and Blane in a stable at a country club. It was like waiting for Godot. He was never going to show up to the ball.

But I liked to think of it more as perfectionism. I mean, who wanted to settle for Mr Goodenough when Mr Right was out there somewhere? Besides, Olly was just mad because he was still yet to kiss anyone besides Cat Walmesley in year six. We thought he might be gay for a bit – he totally hearts *High Society* and knows way too much about the *oeuvre* of Baz Luhrmann – but we borrowed a no-label DVD off his uncles Max and Norman, and nothing moved, let alone the earth.

But, two years later, mine did. Just like I knew it would.

Have you ever wished someone would walk into your life and change everything, just by being alive? That their mere existence would nudge your world off its axis and send everything spinning into a new and brighter orbit?

Well, it happened. On 9 September at 12.35 p.m. Drew Lacey walked into our canteen like Batman and the Joker all packaged up in one neat slick-quiffed, check-shirted, wry-smiling Rockabilly God. His brown eyes met my baby blues as he walked past, his cowboy boots clacking on the Coke-stained concrete, and in that instant I fell in love.

If I could have written the perfect boy, it would have been him. He radiated intrigue and boredom in equal measure, and with a determination bordering on the Olympic. The way he stood outside the chemistry lab, his shoulders leaning against the Dulux orange, bouncing a tennis ball off the wall like he was Newman in the cooler in *The Great Escape*, made my heart ache with want.

Olly said my chances, on a scale of one to The Sure Thing, were nil. Because Charlie Patel saw him kissing Lily Dean on the football pitch and he had his hand up her mini kilt and his tongue so far down her throat it was like he was trying to eat her alive. I said it was just a kiss. And not even a pretty one. But Olly said even if it was just a kiss, I'd still have to wait for the Triple As – Amber, Alexa and August – to have their share. Those girls swapped boyfriends like they swapped cheap earrings. No one seemed to know who was dating who, and maybe it didn't even matter.

Don't get me wrong, Olly didn't put me at the bottom of the list. I was way ahead of Verity King and Emily Button. I even pipped Hannah Holden, who had DDs and a daddy who owned a drug company. But Olly had to say that. That was what best friends did. They held your hand when you were scared, and held your hair back when you were sick.

They told you the truth, but couched it in a little white lie.

But like I said, I was good at waiting.

So I waited. And I clocked up Drew moments like I was collecting pennies in a jar.

I had seven.

1. That first look in the canteen. The opening credits. The beginning of everything.
2. The time he brushed my shoulder in the crowd at the vending machine. Olly said Stan Havory pushed him and it was an accident. Nothing more. But even though he barely touched me, I felt it in every inch of my body. And that was no accident.

3. The time I opened my locker and a lifetime of kitsch and Johnny Cash CDs fell out. And while Lily and the Triple As stood there laughing like Disney hyenas, Drew knelt down on one knee and handed me a purple-headed troll like it was a Tiffany diamond.

4. The time our lab partners both got the flu and Mrs Pennington said we might as well buddy up than waste sodium nitrate. The significance of "chemistry" was not lost on me.

5. The time in French when Madame Leblanc asked everyone to name a Paris landmark and we said "Jim Morrison's grave" as one voice, and he jinxed me.

6. The time he stood behind me in the canteen queue and asked me if I was harbouring suicidal thoughts when I picked the macaroni. I said I was the kind of girl who liked to live on the edge. Which would have worked a whole lot better if

I hadn't also had a carton of skimmed and a cookie on my tray. But the line was a good one and he knew it.

7. The time he bust the G on his six-string in the common room one Friday lunch and I gave him a spare from my duffel bag. He'd been playing chart cheese to Lily. A ballad about beauty and the blues. But after he got the string he switched straight to Johnny Cash. My song. Our song.

Seven moments over seven months. Straws, Olly said. And I was clutching at them. But then in the eighth month Aphrodite and Venus and all those other goddesses of love looked down on me. And I went from seven to heaven in one week.

It was a week of fortuity. Of fates colliding and fortune smiling. Serendipity, I said. Only without John Cusack or Kate Beckinsale or the glove counter at Bloomingdale's.

On Monday Amber told August who told

Alexa who told Drew that Lily had kissed Finn Shakespeare in the back row of the Odeon on Saturday night.

On Tuesday Lily was crying in the upper girls' bathroom at first break and it was clear from the conversation I caught from stall two that this was not just a bad time of the month or a broken nail.

On Wednesday Amber's aunt got cooties, aka colon disease, and her parents flew out of town for the weekend to be at her bedside. Amber decided not to go on the grounds that she had an algebra exam on Tuesday next, a full drinks cabinet, and an overwhelming urge to have a bunch of randoms chuck up in her downstairs toilet while listening to overloud R 'n' B.

On Thursday Charlie Patel, who was August's flavour of the month, invited Olly to the party during AV club and told him he could plus one.

And then on Friday I hit jackpot. I was in the canteen making Sophie's choice between the lasagne and the chicken pie, when someone behind me said, "Just eeny meeny miny mo them. That way you can blame fate instead of yourself when you're praying to the porcelain god by home time."

I didn't need to turn round to know it was him. His voice was sand and glue, like Dylan's. A low, cool drawl. And I smelt him. Cigarettes and Doublemint and possibility. But I did turn, and I smiled. And he smiled right back.

And then it happened. He said, "So you're going to Amber's, right?"

I said, "Maybe I am; maybe I'm not. But I'm surprised you are. Aren't you *persona non grata* round the mock Tudor mansions these days?"

And he laughed. A proper, guileless laugh. "I think Amber weighed up the odds and decided Lily's comfort and convenience were worth less than a free crate of beer."

Which wasn't generosity on his part. I mean, his dad owned a chain of off-licences. But I got his point. I always got his point. "She'd never make the maths club," I dead-panned.

"Not with those thighs," he batted back.

And then I realized we could be playing safe net

shots for a while here. So I took a risk. I hit a smash, hard and true. "So maybe I'll see you there."

"Not if I see you first." And he winked. He actually winked. Not a cheesy game-show host one, but an "I have seen *Stand by Me* and know it's in your Top Ten Films of All Time list, even though Kiefer Sutherland is in it and he gives you the hives" nudge.

And then it was done. The moment was over. Because a dinner lady in a pink hairnet was telling me to hurry up and Charlie had pushed in between us to get the last piece of pie. But it didn't matter. Because those few words and seconds were worth a cold plate of pasta. Because I knew he knew. I knew he got it. And got me. And that Saturday night would be the scene I'd been waiting for. Saturday night, in a bedroom on Mulholland Drive, would be our first kiss.

But like any great movie kiss, it was all in the set-up. And I had scripted it like a skinny-jeaned Scorcese.

Costume was easy. Emerald green fifties prom dress. Trusty Chuck Taylors. My mother's Chanel No. 5. Dietrich meets Marilyn, with a little bit of Juno thrown in as a nod to the indies. Like me, but better. A 3D technicoloured remake of a much-loved black and white classic. For props I travelled light. Just my smile, and my guitar. Because I didn't want to be the girl nodding and swaying while some wannabe Cobain strummed out sub-Nirvana grunge on a swing chair. I played a mean "Folsom Prison Blues" and I wanted Drew to know it.

And dialogue – well, I knew it word for word. I had lines from Bergman and Hitchcock, and a whole scene from Zeffirelli down pat. Of course, this would rely on there being a balcony some-where, but at Amber's house I figured this would be a real possibility.

But like all great movie plans, there was a hitch. A villain who twirls his moustache at the eleventh hour and sends it all to hell in a handcart.

I just never figured mine would be Olly.

"I can't face it," he said, when I called round to collect him.

"What?" I asked.

"The whole thing. The shit sound system and the cheap shots."

"But you *have* to come," I said, pulling his jacket off the hook. "You have a key line. The scene won't work without you. You're the sidekick, the buddy, who gets the best lines and the laughs."

"But not the girl," he said.

I shrugged. And then he lost it. Went scary crazy in a monologue worthy of De Niro.

"What if I don't want to be a bit player in the big movie of your so-called life any more?" he spat. "Christ, it's not even a movie. It's a pathetic little made-for-TV drama. A soap. You're not Cathy and he's not Heathcliff. He's just another MTV extra who hands it out to anyone with tits and a credit card."

And just when I thought it was over, he came back for a grand finale.

"Oh, and don't kid yourself. There isn't going

to be a movie kiss. At best you'll go straight to third base on a pile of coats in the corner."

Nobody puts me in a corner, I thought.

But the door had slammed. He was gone.

And *scene*.

And I stood on his doorstep, the rain beginning to fall. And I wanted to go home. I wanted to sit on my bed with my graffitied wall behind me like Duckie while Morrissey begged to get what he wants, this time.

But I wasn't Duckie. I wasn't best supporting. I was the leading lady. I was Marilyn and Marlene and Molly. I didn't need him, I just needed myself. My guts, my guitar and my cute dress.

In any case, Olly might miss his line, and mess up the whole scene.

But in the end, I managed to do that all by myself.

Drew's on the deck with Charlie and Stan. They're jamming to – my, oh my – "Smells Like Teen

Spirit", an appreciation society of preppy and perky wannabe princesses nodding in time like those plastic rear-window dogs, not really hearing it. Not getting it.

I don't do the groupie thing. Not my style. I wait until he sees me. Then I turn and walk, real slow, back into the house, onto my set. And I wait.

There's no balcony. Which is a huge oversight given the frankly staggering views across the rooftops. Mr Barrett was missing a trick when he designed this late twentieth-century monstrosity. But there's a fake Tiffany lamp, and a bed and a poster of Audrey. And I can work with these. I'm a professional, after all. And in the end the set blurs into the background, because the camera focus is on my face as I hear the door handle turn, and I dampen the G chord and look up.

It's him. Of course it's him. His hair slick with wax, his mouth pulling into that catlike grin.

"Nice notes, Johnny," he says, and leans back against the door, clicking it shut behind him.

God, even the way he leans is beautiful. He

could say nothing, do nothing but lean, and I would be mesmerized.

"You took your time," I say.

"Well, I'm worth the wait," he replies.

I falter. Because that's just a tad too confident. He's supposed to be endearingly nervous. Because it's not just going to be a kiss; it's going to be the start of something. Of everything. But I take the material I'm given and I work with it. I rise, letting the guitar fall onto the duvet, and I walk towards him, my lips parted, waiting to say my next line.

But he's already coming at me, and before I can get the words out his mouth is on mine, and he's pushing me back, towards the bed.

The earth isn't moving.

I stumble, falling onto my guitar, a discordant minor filling the room.

There are no violins.

His weight pushes me down as his hand pushes heavy green lace up.

A thousand doves do not fly to the heavens.

And as his fingers reach towards the forbidden,

it hits me: John Hughes is not directing this scene. *I* am not even directing this scene. He is. His raging hormone-fuelled, Internet-porn-filled, lame frat movie brain is in charge. And I know how this one ends. And it's not going to be with a happy ever after.

I twist my head so his tongue slides, doglike, across my cheek. "Get off me."

"What the—" he protests.

But I am incredulous. And incredible. Unscripted now, but the lines keep coming.

"What did you think this was going to be? You were supposed to be the hero. The James Mason or Jimmy Dean. But you're just another two-bit dime store hoodlum like the rest."

But my words are wasted. Falling like ripe cherries on concrete.

"What are you on?" He stares at me. His brown eyes black with fury and broken pride. Not getting me. In any sense. "Lily was right about you. Total freaking nut job." He stands, straightening his T-shirt. Making sure his hair and ego are intact.

I say nothing. I have nothing left *to* say. Nothing that fits. Nothing that I could speak aloud without the sobs starting. So I stand, and walk towards the door, in a cloud of Chanel and quiet desperation.

"Where are you going?" he demands.

"Nowhere. Somewhere. Stardust Freaking Avenue."

Cut to me at the punch bowl downing a plastic Incredibles cupful of courage.

Cut to the jacuzzi, where Drew is half naked with August, a *ten minutes later* caption fading in and out at the bottom of the screen.

Cut to me throwing stones at Olly's window. A guitar strapped across a ripped and ragged prom dress. Snot mixing with salt tears on my skin.

"Wake up," I plead. "Olly, you have to wake up. I'm sorry. You were right. I'm a bad person, Olly."

"You're not bad."

The voice comes from the doorway. I turn and see him, the light from the hallway a halo around him, like a Hallmark Card angel.

"You're not asleep?" I sniff.

"Couldn't." He shrugs.

I nod. I know. "I'm sorry," I repeat. "It... He—"

"I know," he cuts in. Saving me. Like he always does.

And so I let him. I let him put his arms around me, and hold me, and tell me it's going to be all right. That tonight doesn't matter. That it will happen. The kiss.

I pull back and look at him, into him. "When?" I ask.

He smiles. "If this was a movie, you know what would happen, right?"

"No," I lie.

"If you won't say it, I will."

My heart beats louder. But steady now. Not the flutter and fear I felt with Drew. But something stronger. I dare him. "So say it."

"Fine," he says, his eyes still on mine. "I would say, 'It's you. It's always been you.' And then—"

"I'd say, 'It just took a while to know it,'" I continue.

"And then?"

"And then…" I say. "And then—"

"We'd kiss," he finishes.

I feel my heart skip like the cliché it is. "We would?" I whisper.

But I know it. I know he's right. "We would," I repeat. The question gone.

I move towards him. Then stop, pull back. "Wait," I say. "What if I don't feel anything? What if the world doesn't stop and there are no violins and stuff?"

"Then we go back to doing our double act. We are Bonnie and Clyde."

"Tango and Cash," I add.

"Laurel and Hardy." He smiles.

But it's not funny. Because… "What if we do? Feel something, I mean?"

"I don't know. But that's what's so beautiful about the real world. It's uncharted. There's no script. No plot line. We just see where it takes us."

"Really?"

"Really."

And I know it's over. The talking. The waiting.

I know that the next scene up is the biggie.

And I close my eyes, and move forward. Until I can feel his breath on my cheek. Until I can feel his lips on mine.

Until the earth moves.

And *scene*.

— ALL OF A — SUDDEN

Adele Parks

Whilst standing in an endless line for tickets at Victoria Station, it hits me that, likely as not, right now Oliver Sutton and Zoe Clarkson will be deciding between beach and pool. The most exciting decision I have in front of me is whether to buy a tuna and cucumber sandwich from Boots or wait until we get to Brighton and have lunch there.

"I'm so excited. It's going to be such a laugh!" says Jaz.

I wish her excitement was infectious – it normally is – but today I'm immune. I sigh and look down at my scruffy rucksack. Life's so unfair. I bet Zoe Clarkson has a set of matching luggage, with wheels and everything. Besides the emotional baggage, I am travelling light, because a day trip to Brighton simply does not require the same amount of stuff as a fortnight's dream holiday in the Maldives. All I've packed is a few gossipy, glossy magazines, full of pictures of film stars without their shirts on. Jaz hates this sort of mag – she says they're boring – but she let me buy three of them today because she's trying to cheer me up.

"What do you think they're doing now?" I ask her.

"Who?"

"Who!" I'm startled by my bessie's ignorance. "*Who?* Him. Him and *her*. Who else? *Oliver* and that Zoe Clarkson." I spit out her name like a curse. It nearly chokes me. I'm gutted. My heart actually hurts.

"Dunno," Jaz mumbles with a shrug. She means, "Don't care" but, as I said, she's trying to be patient with me. "Look, I'm in love. Well, almost. I'm in like, something at least. I do get it," she says, and then she squeezes my arm in a gesture of solidarity.

She does not get it.

She and Freddie McNeil have been on two dates and they are not suited. They have nothing in common. Freddie McNeil is a total maths geek, and Jaz's idea of complicated maths is working out if she can afford a new eyeliner, a cappuccino *and* the bus home. I'm not having a go; it's just true. She's really into biology and history – now *there* she shines. Go on, ask her about genetic diseases or any of the King Georges and she's a marvel, but ask her about geometry and is she impressive? Not so much. She was totally freaked out when she and Freddie went ice skating and he tried to calculate the area of the rink by estimating the radius, then doing something with pi. She said to me, and I quote, "We weren't even eating pies!"

I decide not to bring this up, nor that he blushes when he speaks to her (not hot!), or that I think she only went out with him because he asked her and she didn't like to hurt his feelings by saying no. Instead, I reply as tactfully as I can. "Yes, but our situations are very different."

"True, I've actually gone out with Freddie," she replies harshly, leaving me wondering why I bothered being tactful to her.

It *is* a sad fact that I wasn't ever Oliver's girlfriend. We never actually went on a single date. There were obstacles. At first I thought those obstacles were surmountable and the sort to be expected in any real romance – I mean, Romeo and Juliet had loads of obstacles (actually, they may not be the best example) – but it turned out the obstacles were for real. He's older than me, he works in our school library and he has a girlfriend. I perhaps could have got past the first two, but the third one is a deal breaker.

I found out about Zoe Clarkson the day we broke up for the holidays. She came into the library at the end of the day, when I just happened to be there (I often happen to be in there – for obvious reasons), and she was all giggly and pretty. Oliver introduced us and mentioned that she'd popped in to check out a travel guide because they were off on this amazing once-in-a-lifetime holiday.

Jaz thinks he might be planning on proposing to Zoe, because that's the sort of thing that happens in the Maldives. I suppose it does. Either way Zoe and the holiday were indisputable evidence that Oliver has not been thinking of me in the way I've been thinking of him, and that he probably does think I have a genuine interest in the Dewey decimal system. Love doesn't make sense and isn't fair. That much I know to be true. The fact is I adore him; haven't been able to think about anyone or anything else for three months now. He's kind and funny. He has loads of interests and he's just not *daft* like practically every other boy I know.

"He's a god in my eyes."

"I get it. He looks like Logan Lerman, but, Immy, he's totally ancient. Probably twenty-three. And he's a *librarian*." She says the word "librarian" the way other people might say "leper".

"I thought he was the One, you know."

"How can he be the One? You're fourteen."

"Technically."

"What other way is there to be fourteen?"

"What I mean is, although I am fourteen, I'm very mature. My nana always says I was born old."

"I'd keep quiet about that if I were you. And you're continually falling in love with unobtainables. It's embarrassing."

"I am not *continually* falling in love with unobtainables."

"Yes, you are."

"Like who?"

"Like Zac Efron."

"Well, everyone is in love with him."

"Yes, but not everyone really believes they're going to marry him. Then there was Troy's dad. That was just gross."

"Why? He's not married to Troy's mum any more."

"He's a *dad*, Immy! Then there was Mr Lowell, our PE teacher."

"He's fit."

"He's a *teacher*! Then there was Chloe's brother."

"He's not a teacher."

"He's gay. And, finally, Harry Kepal."

"OK, he's not a dad or a teacher, nor is he gay."

"Immy, he's in prison for car theft. There's a barbed wire fence between the two of you. If that doesn't say unobtainable, I don't know what does."

Finally we're at the front of the queue. We buy our tickets, check the timetable and then leg it so we can make the 10.25 a.m. train. We find an emptyish carriage and stare down a woman and her toddler son who are keen to bag the last couple of table seats facing the direction of travel (the table is essential, so we can spread out our magazines). The seats are ours – it's a small victory but it cheers me. I plan to pass the journey staring out of the window, watching the houses and fields rush by. I think this is symbolic: life is passing me by. I make the mistake of sharing my observation with Jaz.

She replies, "I don't know about symbolic, more like shambolic. You shouldn't be letting anything pass you by. We're young. It's all ours for the taking. Do you know what I think is wrong with you?"

"I have an awful feeling you're about to tell me."

"You're shy."

"What?" This is nonsense. I'm known as a bit of a loudmouth, a definite laugh and chatty to the point of indiscreet, hasn't Jaz just said as much herself?

"Or, more accurately," she adds, turning to me. She's wearing a really serious expression that freaks me because Jaz doesn't really do serious, "afraid and – don't have a fit – insecure."

"What?" I repeat, outraged.

"That's why you go after blokes you know you don't stand a chance with because then you'll never have to get to the nitty-gritty bits of a relationship. If you actually fancied a boy your own age you might have to speak to him or – horror of horrors – kiss him."

I glare at Jaz. She's been absolutely unbearable since she kissed Freddie McNeil and (unbelievably) enjoyed it. She thinks she knows everything about everything, or at least everything important, like about boys. It is true that I've often enjoyed the fact that Jaz knows me so well. We've laughed that it sometimes seems like she knows me better than I know myself, but she is wrong about this! Isn't she? Anyway, I'm not going to give her the satisfaction of agreeing with her, even if she is right. Which she isn't. At least, she's probably not.

My face is aflame. It's a terrible mix of indignation, fury and shame. The thing is she *might* be right and, if she is, I hate her for pointing it out. Well, hate her and love her at the same time, you know? The way you do with a best friend. I mean, it's good that she cares enough to try and show me where I'm going wrong, but it's still the ultimate in humiliation.

The train pulls up in Clapham Junction and I focus my attention on a group of boys larking around on the platform. At least it's something to look at until my fury and indignation at Jaz subside. They're all young, stupid and generally pretty spotty, but I have to admit that their overall impression is buoyed up by an overwhelming aura of self-confidence. Jaz is looking in the same direction and quickly assesses the five lads.

"Three, six, six, eight, and I can't tell with the last guy as he has his back to us," she says.

I instantly get what she's talking about. She's giving them marks out of ten. It's insensitive and a bit immature, and we'd hate it if boys did it to us but, as we're pretty sure they do, we've overcome our scruples and now follow the motto of "If you can't beat them, join them." Oliver was a clear ten, but Jaz would never give him more than six because she said marks had to be subtracted for his age and career choice.

The boy that she awarded three out of ten has a face that only his mother could love, although he looks happy enough and is repeatedly throwing a tennis ball in the air and assertively catching it. If he's good at sports, or funny, his score will go up to a strong six. If he's clever as well, then he'll be a seven.

I am not sure boys are as generous when they are sizing up girls, but they should be. It's about the whole deal, isn't it? Being pretty is great but being funny, clever, musical or sporty should count for something too. My score is somewhere between a three and an eight depending on who you ask. I say three; Jaz says eight and then reminds me I'm fairly good on the guitar and I draw well. She says I'm funny even when I don't mean to be, but she's probably just being nice because she has to be, she's my best friend. Jaz is a nine but thinks she's about a four.

The two guys Jaz has awarded sixes are only average-looking, but they're clean and trendy enough. The one that is a clear eight has all-American good looks, but he keeps flicking his hair and checking his reflection in his mates' sunglasses, which suggests he's very aware that clear eights are extremely hard to come by.

Our carriage pulls up parallel to where they're

stood. I'm stuck between willing them into my carriage – which is empty now except for an old couple with a flask and egg sandwiches, and the disgruntled mother and toddler – and desperately hoping that they'll sit elsewhere. The motivation for these opposing wishes is the same. If they sit near us I'm pretty sure Jaz will see this as an opportunity for me to talk to boys my own age and, importantly, talk appropriately. She probably won't want me to tell them about how in love I am with Oliver Sutton.

They choose our carriage. I daren't look up, but I sense that four of the boys settle across the aisle while one, mortifyingly, plonks himself opposite us.

"*Bonjour,*" he says firmly.

French?

I can't resist. I look up.

Bang! Eleven out of ten.

The most sensational-looking boy *ever* is smiling at me. He's literally breathtaking. Even sitting down, I can tell he's quite tall with broad shoulders and slim hips. He has scruffy dark hair that falls over his cobalt blue eyes. I can't believe it; he's a little bit like Oliver Sutton, in so much as Oliver also has dark hair and blue eyes, but – and the thought is an extraordinary one for me to even consider – he might just be better-looking than Oliver, because his hairstyle is much cooler and, I suppose I can admit it now, Oliver does wear unfashionable shirts. I mean, he has to – his job requires him to be formal. But still.

The boy smiles. The smile ignites his entire face and, helpless to resist, I smile shyly back. Under the table his knee briefly brushes mine.

"Sorry," I mumble, mortified in case he thinks I have deliberately put my leg in his way.

"*Excusez-moi,*" he says with a beam.

My stomach leaps into my throat. I didn't know that was even biologically possible.

"So you're French," comments Jaz, as though speaking to him is the easiest thing in the world. My tongue is glued to the roof of my mouth and I very much doubt it's going to move ever again.

How could I find the words fit for this guy?

"Oui. Je suis français," he replies with another grin.

His mates all snigger. They are not French, you can tell. Their hair and clothes don't have that Continental sophistication, so I guess they are sniggering at the word *"oui"*. So mature, not. The boys in my class never grow tired of that sad joke either.

"I em on an exchange programme," he adds, confirming my summation. His accent is unbelievable. So cool and yet, well, so hot. I still can't think of anything to say; I'm just worried he'll be able to hear my heart beating or my blood rushing around my body in a frenzy.

"Interesting," comments Jaz, as though it is just that, rather than earth-shattering, which clearly would be a more accurate description. "Where. Are. You. From?" she asks.

"Paris," he replies.

"Oh, Paris," I gasp. The thought of Paris catapults me out of my silent stupor. Paris is the most romantic city in the world. Ever. No arguments. Full stop. Not that I've ever been there but I can totally imagine it. It's full of endless fountains, countless elegant lamp posts, innumerable tall clean trees, dozens upon dozens of grand cream buildings and wide avenues. *"Paris est si belle,"* I enthuse.

"Parlez-vous français?"

"Oui!" I say with an eagerness that surprises me. It's actually one of my favourite subjects. *"Je parle un peu de français."*

One of his mates leans across the aisle and says, "Very impressive but he has to practise his English, so no more French, OK?"

"Oh, OK." I'm strangely disappointed. I'm not sure why but I was looking forward to speaking French.

"You have to speak slowly. If you go too fast he doesn't get it," the boy adds.

"Right."

My disappointment vanishes as the lovely French guy shrugs and holds his hand out across the table for me to shake. How mature is that? There's no way an English boy would ever do anything as sophisticated. I reach for his hand and carefully shake it. Literally there's a bolt of electricity between us. I've heard people say things like that before. I've never really believed it before, but it is true! Lightning slices through me. I don't want to linger too long with his hand in mine but somehow I want to communicate that yes, yes, I will marry him.

He beams. "I em Pierre."

"Imogen."

"It's beautiful."

I don't even care that the other boys are falling off their seats and choking on their own laughter.

I know Jaz might think that technically Pierre is just another unobtainable. Admittedly he's French, has limited English and he's only going to be in the country for a few more days, the duration of the half-term holiday probably. However, on the plus side, he is at least my age and so she seems happy enough to allow me to chat to him.

She amuses herself with talking to his English mates. She's arguing a fine point about last night's football match. Something about whether Rooney really deserved a yellow card or not.

The good thing about talking to someone with limited English is that I don't try to be too clever. I'm not gossipy, or gobby, or indiscreet, or tongue-tied (at least I'm not once I've recovered from my initial shock at just how gorgeous Pierre is). I don't have to be cool so there aren't any awful gaps in the conversation. In fact, I chat more freely than I would with any other boy I'd just met. Because Pierre is struggling with the language he doesn't say much, but what he does say seems honest and straightforward. I guess it's hard to play games in a second language. He tells me I have a lovely smile and pretty ears! I can't tell if he is flirting with me or if he's simply unilaterally charming because he's French. It doesn't really matter either way. I allow myself to relax into the conversation and have fun. Knowing he understands little allows Jaz and me to keep swapping quick, garbled asides. We have agreed that he's uber-cute and that I should do my best to get him to spend the day with us in Brighton.

It's a beautiful day and the good weather has made everyone want to dash to the coast, so when we arrive at Brighton it's heaving. No one actually says we should hang out together, but it's silently accepted that we will be a gang. Pierre's mates walk behind us, while Pierre walks next to Jaz and me. I start to act like some sort of tour guide pointing out local sights and delicacies (if you can call a plate of rock shaped like an English breakfast a delicacy). I find that for once I'm not struggling to think of what to say, therefore I'm not saying crazy stuff and – if the look on Pierre's face is anything to go by – I might just be interesting. But then he is easily pleased; he even appears charmed by the kiss-me-quick hats.

We wander through the Lanes, past the Pavilion and along the pier. It's the dreamiest day ever. We ride the fairground attractions and I notice that Pierre always manages the seating arrangement so that he's sat next to me. With his jean-clad thigh pushed up against mine, I completely forget that the waltzers usually make me feel sick.

We have so much fun shooting targets to try to win soft toys, scooping up rubber ducks and then buying doughnuts and ice creams. We share them – we actually feed them to one another, the way people do in films. I think it's a French thing. And they taste so good, better than anything I've ever tasted before. Then we head to one of the dozens of grotty cafes that serve Coke and greasy chips with fried fish. Normally I'm really careful about what I eat in front of boys – I don't ever want to look like a pig – but Pierre keeps saying how great it is that I'm not faddy (pronounced *fadeeeee*) and so I join him and the others as they dive into gigantic portions.

Afterwards, the boys club together to buy a Frisbee and a soft football. We laugh and play on the beach all afternoon. It's pebbled rather than the white sands that I know Oliver and Zoe will be treading on in the Maldives on their holiday of a lifetime. But that doesn't matter. I am having so much fun that suddenly I feel totally stupid for ever thinking I should be the one on holiday with Oliver. I am right where I ought to be, sat between my best mate and a cute French boy, watching the waves lap the shore. Pierre grins at me and I hope he's thinking what I'm thinking. It's the best day of my life.

Eventually, inevitably, the sun starts to set but the beach is still pretty busy. We watch people round up their cross kids – tired and burnt they cry and argue with their siblings. Older couples are walking their dogs. They've already been back to their hotels to shower and change into their pastel shirts and summer dresses. It's getting late. Jaz is checking the timetable; we'll have to get a train back to London soon. My dad is picking us up at the station and he'll have a sense of humour failure if we're late.

Pierre shivers.

"Are you cold?" I ask.

"Before you say to your friend I am hot?" he says, confusion flowing from him.

I blush; I hadn't meant him to hear that and I certainly can't explain it. Luckily he doesn't expect me to. He smiles and then rubs his hands up and down my arms as if I'm the one who is cold. It feels so good. His fingers move up to my shoulders and then my neck. I close my eyes and therefore feel, rather than see, him move closer and closer until his lips gently touch mine.

It's explosive. It's vibrant, definitive, exhilarating. All I can think is that I'm no longer pleased this boy is one of my unobtainables, as Jaz likes to call them. I wish we could talk some more. Endlessly. I wish he was staying in this country. I wish I had time to get to know him. The kiss is sweet; it's exciting; it's perfect; it's thrilling.

As I pull away I fully expect Pierre to look as content and excited as I do. For the first time in my life I am actually expecting a boy's feelings to mirror my own, rather than just hoping and praying they will, so I am shocked to see that he doesn't look excited or thrilled. He looks guilty and miserable. I can't think why. I know the kiss was a good one. It's impossible that it felt so wonderful for me and not good for him, so what can possibly be wrong?

"I'm sorry. I feel terrible. It wasn't supposed to go this far. It's over," says Pierre as he abruptly pulls away and strides off.

Suddenly I'm aware of his mates whooping and laughing. I'd forgotten about their existence. I turn and see them point and jeer, like stupid boys do. Jaz looks as confused as I am. What's going on? What went wrong?

Humiliation threatens to drown me. This is worse than anything I have ever experienced with Harry Kepal, Oliver Sutton or anyone. I knew getting involved with a real boy was a hideous risk. This rejection coming right on the back of the sweetness of his kiss is a thousand times worse than mooning over a guy who doesn't know I care about him taking his girlfriend to the Maldives.

"Let's go!" I yell at Jaz. I grab my bag and start to march off in what I hope is the general direction of the station and, more importantly, is in the opposite direction to where Pierre went.

"Wait up." Jaz is by my side in an instant. She keeps pace with me, even though I'm striding. I'm keen to put some distance between me and the taunting boys. "What happened?" she asks.

"I don't know."

"I thought you were getting on."

"We were. He kissed me." I just can't say it. I daren't articulate my biggest fear. Did I do it wrong? I don't have to; Jaz knows me well enough.

"He looked as though he was into you."

"I am." We both turn suddenly towards Pierre's voice. It *is* his voice although it's different. "I am really into you, but—"

"Where's your accent gone?" demands Jaz.

"I'm not Pierre. I'm Peter. I'm not French. I'm—"

"A joke!" Jaz is there a moment before I am.

"My friends dared me."

"You pig."

"No, it's not as bad as it sounds."

I can't imagine how this can sound anything

other than terrible and I have a big imagination. I glare at him.

"We didn't do it to be mean. I was practising."

"What?" Jaz and I yell our indignation in unison.

Pierre/Peter, whatever he's called, looks horrified. "No, I don't mean *you* were practice. I was practising talking to girls, in general."

"You are unbelievable!" yells Jaz, and she slips a protective arm round me.

"Oh no. You see, I'm no good at this. That's the point." He groans and runs his hands through his hair. He actually looks as though he wants to pull it out. I wish I could say I was no longer attracted to him but somehow, despite his nasty trick, I am managing to find his anguish cute. How is that even possible? Will I ever learn? "I wasn't out to deceive you. I didn't expect it to go on longer than the train journey. But, well, when we got here, I didn't want to leave you…" He stumbles over his words and I notice a slight flush hover around his cheekbones; it could be the sun or he could be blushing. I was wrong, a guy blushing when he talks to you is actually very cool.

"What do you mean?" I ask. I think I know, but I want to hear him say it.

"Well, I like you. I didn't mean to make a fool of you or trick you."

"We're out of here," says Jaz firmly and loyally. She knows I can't stand being messed around – which girl can? And she knows I live in fear of making a fool of myself. "You're not her type. She only kissed you because she thought you were an unobtainable."

Peter looks ashamed and upset. "What's an unobtainable?"

"Librarian, teacher, someone's dad, gay guys, jailbirds, French dudes."

"That's your type?" Now he looks distraught. Hearing it said out loud, I'm pretty distraught too. I sound clinically insane. "What can I say? At least I don't pretend to be French."

"I only did that because—" He breaks off, takes a deep breath and then spits out, "I'm lousy at talking to girls. I get tongue-tied. My mates thought that taking on a different persona might help me relax."

"What?" demands Jaz.

I'm wondering how such a cute guy can possibly have a confidence issue, and I don't know whether to trust him or believe him, but then he adds, "I guess I'm shy, a bit afraid that I'll say something that makes me sound like an idiot."

It's too raw to be anything other than honesty. Jaz and I share a glance and I can see she believes him too.

"Yeah, pretending to be French doesn't give us that impression at all," says Jaz, but she's smiling. It's impossible not to smile at Pierre/Peter's embarrassed but cute and a tiny bit hopeful grin. He hasn't taken his eyes off me. He's no doubt pleased that Jaz looks as though she might forgive him, but I have a feeling that what he wants to know most is whether *I* understand him.

"Once I'd started the stupid French thing I didn't know how to tell you that I wasn't French. I thought you might lose interest."

"I've been thinking about the types of guys I'm usually attracted to," I say.

"Yes?"

"And all of a sudden I'm prepared to review." Peter looks hopeful; Jaz looks curious. "I'll add pathological liars to that list, or maybe guys with identity crises, or—"

I don't get a chance to finish, because Peter pulls me close and silences me with a kiss.

DOG DAYS

Madhvi Ramani

"*You're my desert rain, You cool me down, ease my pain.*"

I turn the radio off.

"Oi! I was listening to that," pants Mum.

She's smoking a ciggy while on the treadmill. She's on this new health thing. *New Body, New Mind, New Me,* she says – but I suppose old habits die hard. Not that I'm complaining. At least she's trying.

"I'm off," I say.

"OK. And, Leona, love, make sure you eat something. Breakfast is the most important meal of the day, you know. There's crisps on the counter."

I smile and nod. Like I said, she's trying.

"And turn the radio back on!"

I flip the switch. The lyrics of the song follow me out: "*You're my desert rose, As you unfurl, my love grows...*" Seven weeks at number-one. Whoever's buying it should be shot.

I walk down the cool, dark stairwell and out into the car park. The sun gleams off the satellite dishes and concrete blocks around me. Rows of square windows shimmer in the heat. Everything looks washed out. Even the sky, which should be blue, looks like a pair of jeans that's been through the machine too many times.

Dog days, they're calling them. Globally warmed days, more like. But no one cares about that. All that matters to people is that they can lie around half naked and get a tan. Not me. I'm so pale I don't even tan. I just turn red – the colour of my hair – and then my skin starts to peel. It's not pretty. And you won't catch me in a bikini. Not with my scars. Lying around in the park all summer is boring anyway. I'd choose the animal sanctuary any day.

The only flash of colour on my way there is the

spaceship sprayed across the side of the bookies. It's tagged "WallBreaker" – our very own graffiti artist. Like most of his stuff, it's a mad blend of colours – purple, pink, silver, orange. But its doorway is pure black, which makes you think there's an actual hole in the wall and that any minute, an alien is going to slither out onto the high street.

I'm walking down the hall to the morning meeting when I see it. A pit bull. Amber eyes darting, claws skittering on the tiles, barking its head off. It's pulling at its lead, dragging Faith – the vet who runs the sanctuary – behind it. I stumble back and press myself against the wall. I can smell the dog as it passes, see its incisors and the inside of its mouth, glistening pink.

It's only after the dog's gone, and I breathe a sigh of relief, that I realize the wall I am standing against doesn't really feel like a wall. It's breathing. I turn and find myself facing a guy about my age, with caramel-coloured skin and curly hair springing out of his head in all directions. His chest is wide and flat, but it's definitely no wall. His dark eyes study me.

"All right?" he says.

My skin starts to burn, and I know I'm going red. I nod and walk away without looking back, but I can still sense him, leaning against the wall, watching me go.

Faith introduces him at the morning meeting.

"We have a new volunteer! This is Dominic. He'll be here for…" But as usual, she doesn't finish her sentence. She just turns and gives him a mini applause.

Dear God, I think, looking at Faith's pregnant belly, *you're going to have the most embarrassing mum ever.*

Dominic smiles and sits down.

I recall something I saw in Faith's office a couple of weeks ago and it hits me that Dominic is not a normal volunteer like the rest of us. It's supposed to be confidential, but Faith always leaves papers all over her desk, so you can't help but read them. He's a criminal, here on a community-service order.

"Any other business, or … or…" Faith says at the end of the meeting.

"Yeah. The pit bull that came in this morning – are you going to put it down?" I ask.

Pit bulls are illegal, so they have to be put down, but the sanctuary has a *no kill* policy.

"Oh no, Leona! I just examined it. It's a Staffordshire bull terrier – a Staffie – trained to… No doubt because they can be confused with pit bull terriers, so…" And she's lost her train of thought again.

Over the next week, Dominic and I mark out our separate territories. I watch him sometimes, from the window of the cattery, throwing sticks to the dogs. The tendons in his arm ripple in the sun. He never seems to get bored or impatient. The dogs keep coming back, sticks in mouths, tails wagging, and he keeps throwing. They love him. Then again dogs will drool over anyone who throws them a stick. They're stupid like that. I prefer cats. They don't trust just anyone. That's why, statistically, they suffer less abuse than dogs.

There's no denying that Dominic's ... cute. But I've been volunteering at the sanctuary long enough to know about pheromones. They make the animals do stupid things, like sniff each other's bums. And they were probably responsible for making my mum fall for my dad and get pregnant with me when she was just fifteen. I've made it to the same age without smoking or getting distracted by boys – and I'm not about to start now.

One afternoon Faith calls me into the examination room. It looks like she's prodding a small rock, but as I come closer, I realize it's an intricately patterned shell – except it's cracked and chipped, like a jigsaw puzzle with bits missing. It's a tortoise, with its head and legs tucked inside its shell.

"The children it belonged to tried to get the shell off it like they'd seen on some cartoon. Can you believe the...? Trying to take the shell off a tortoise is like trying to take the skin off a..." she says.

Luckily, the kids only damaged the carapace, which is the very outer layer. We have to patch the shell up, though, so bacteria can't get in and infect it. Faith moulds patches out of this special acrylic material and then I hold them in place while she glues them on. We're about halfway through when Debbie comes in to say that one of the sanctuary's sponsors is on the phone.

"Hold that, I'll be…" Faith says, dropping the tube of glue and leaving.

We wait, the tortoise and me, both still, silent. I can hear Roger the rat grinding his teeth in his cage on the other side of the wall. Rats' teeth never stop growing, so they have to wear them down to control their length.

I begin to wonder if Faith has forgotten about me. She's always forgetting her purse or her keys, or her words, mid-sentence. God knows what's going to happen when the baby comes. I wouldn't be surprised if she leaves it behind in the super-market or forgets to pick it up from nursery.

The door opens. It's Dominic.

"Hey, I just bumped into Faith. She said something about…" He tails off.

Christ, being unable to finish your sentences must be contagious.

"Hold this," I say.

His hands are big, with scrapes and pen marks on them. He has to put them over mine to take my place. I can feel the heat from his body; smell this fruity scent that I recognize from the hallway; see the curve of his biceps beneath his T-shirt. I skirt around him quickly to pick up the glue before I go red again.

Moulding the patches isn't as easy as it looks. We circle each other in silence. Occasionally, one of his curls brushes my forehead as we bend over the shell. After a while, we fall into a rhythm. Finally, we step back and look at our handy work. The shell, once beautiful, is covered with white patches of different sizes and shapes.

I cross my arms over my stomach.

"It's not that bad," he offers.

"I'm never going to make it as a vet."

"Isn't it tricky, being a vet, if you're scared of dogs?"

My first instinct is to deny it, but then I remember the scene in the hallway. He knows. I glare at him and see that he isn't teasing or anything. He's genuinely curious.

"Yeah, I mean, I could specialize, but at some point I'd have to deal with dogs."

"I'll teach you if you like," he says.

I start to shake my head, but something about his steady gaze and dark eyes pulls me in. Maybe it will be all right. Maybe this could be my chance to get over my fear, and make it as a vet.

"OK," I say.

I have no idea why I agreed, because by the next day I'm regretting it. I go about my cage-cleaning duties as usual, then I visit the cats. I play with Dara, a white kitten with only one eye. It's blue. The other eye remains closed, like she's permanently winking. She's my favourite cat. I named her. Sometimes when a new animal comes in you get to name it. I give them proper names, names that you would give human beings, not like Debbie, who gives them silly names like Fluffy and Jelly – or Faith, who gives them Greek names like Psyche and Athena.

It's Dara's lucky day, because I play with her for longer than usual. Then I check on Roger and the tortoise that doesn't have a name yet. According to his notes, he hasn't come out of his shell since he arrived. Finally, I stop at the doorway to the yard where the dogs are kept.

Dominic and Clive the behaviourist stand chatting in the sun. I can hear the dogs panting in the heat. I'm about to turn round and walk off when Dominic looks my way.

"Cool. Leona. You came," he says. The way he smiles and says my name makes my stomach flip.

Clive says he's got a troublemaker to deal with and wanders off. I head towards the kennels with Dominic. As we pass through the yard where the dogs are brought out to play, I feel the urge to bolt it back to the building. I only resist because I don't want him thinking I'm more of a scaredy-cat than he already does.

All of a sudden, we're at the kennels. I study the cracked earth and tufts of yellow grass, hoping that if I don't look at the dogs, they'll ignore me. Fat chance. One of them starts going ballistic and out the corner of my eye, I catch a flash of movement. I look up just as a greyhound pounces at me – but is held back by the fence of its kennel. Dominic is speaking, but all I can hear is the thudding of my heart. I stand there, as taut and trembling as the fence, convinced that any minute now, the fence is going to give in to the weight of the hound.

Somehow we move away from the kennels. I become aware of Dominic's hand, hot and solid, on the small of my back. Warmth spreads to the rest of my body, and by the time we reach the door, I almost feel normal again. He lets his hand drop and studies me, as if I'm some kind of strange creature.

"So?" he says.

I realize he's been talking this entire time, but I haven't been paying attention.

"Yeah," I say vaguely.

"Cool. Catch you at the same time tomorrow then," he says, and goes inside, leaving me alone.

He must think I'm a right weirdo. I don't know why I care anyway. There's no way I'm coming out here again.

I stand for a while, listening to the scuffles and yelps of the dogs. Then I realize something: I've never been able to set foot out here before, and even though the kennels are just over there, I'm calm. The fence didn't crumple. I survived.

Before I leave for the day, I creep up to the terrarium to see if I can catch the tortoise with his head out. What I see surprises me. The tortoise is still hiding under his shell, but Dominic is kneeling over it, holding a thin brush. He's painting it, recreating the original pattern of the shell. I slink away without him noticing.

On the way home, I wonder about him. Dominic.

Curiosity killed the cat, whispers a voice in my head.

At two o'clock the next day, I find myself squinting in the sunlight. As long as the dogs are inside their kennels it will be all right, I tell myself as Dominic and I make our way across the yard. We stick to the middle of the path between the kennels, not getting too close. They're all made of the same wire-mesh fencing and are pretty big, with balls and toys and old bits of furniture in them. The dogs are safely inside with the gates locked, but I still don't like it. I don't like the smell of the dogs, their neediness, the way they rush up to their fences when we approach, wagging their tails, barking, jumping up and down. The Staffie from the hallway snarls.

I concentrate on putting one foot in front of the other. Dominic has an easy walk – slow, with a bounce, as if he's walking to a beat that no one else can hear.

When we reach the end of the path, we walk

back down. I read the boards on each of the kennels. They give the names of the dogs inside: Dolly Parton, John Travolta, Leonard Cohen...

"They all have weird names," I say to Dominic when we get back to the main building.

"Clive names them after famous people," he says. "Oh yeah, Faith said I could name the tortoise."

"Cool. What you gonna call it?"

"I might use Clive's method. I was thinking maybe Jake Blakemore. I liked him in *Infected*."

"Yeah, I loved that film. Except the end."

"Really? That was the best bit."

"It's unrealistic. If a super-virus like that came along all the scientists would die before they found a cure."

"What about *Magna*, did you see that?" he asks.

"Same problem. Realistic until the end. The earth's magnetic field is already changing, and is anyone doing anything about it"

He glances at me sideways through his long black eyelashes and raises his eyebrows.

"Bees are disappearing worldwide," I add, as if that's going to win the argument.

By the end of the week, I think I've got the walk sorted – but then Dominic strolls right up to Marilyn Monroe, a straggly grey and black schnauzer and I'm practically hiding behind his back. It's ridiculous, but I can't help it. He sticks his fingers into the kennel.

"She looks nothing like Marilyn Monroe," I whisper, not wanting to offend her.

"Clive says she's depressed. And so was Marilyn," Dominic explains.

Marilyn lopes over to us and sniffs his fingers.

"See, she doesn't bite," he says, turning to me.

Slowly, I reach out and put my finger through. My hand is shaking. Marilyn looks at it, then sniffs. Her nose is wet against my fingertip.

We do the same with some of the other dogs, going right up to their kennels to say hello. I don't put my fingers into all of the cages. With some, I stand back and watch Dominic play with the dogs. Surprisingly, it's OK. Maybe this whole laid-back vibe Dominic's got going on is affecting me. Or his presence makes me feel safe. Then again it's probably just that the gates are bolted shut.

"What did you think about *Red*?" he asks.

"Yeah, good film."

"Even the end?"

I nod.

"So it's unrealistic when a scientist finds a cure for a virus, but when the earth is dying and there are limited resources, people will have the chance to resettle on a beautiful, untouched planet?"

I look at him to see whether he's having a laugh, but he's not.

"You've got it all wrong," I say. "There is no untouched planet. It's a lie. The government is just blasting people into space to get rid of them. Lottie and Junot aren't going to Planet Red; they're going to die."

"Nah. Planet Red is out there, and Lottie and Junot are living on it. I can just feel it," he says.

I look at his wide, trusting eyes and almost get sucked in. I shake my head. He can *feel* it? What rubbish.

I hear Mum chanting before I even get through the door. *"I am confident. I am worthy of true love. I am a beloved child of the universe."* She's sitting cross-legged on the living-room floor.

"Leona, your dad called," she says.

Coldness creeps through me, despite the thirty-degree heat. It's been a good year since we've heard from him.

"What did he want?" I ask.

"Nothing. I don't know. I said I didn't want to talk to him and hung up. Pulled the wire out the socket, for good measure."

Relief washes over me. She's never done that before.

On the way to the sanctuary the next day I glance at the spaceship, and for a moment, I see it differently. Instead of believing that something terrible is about to emerge from that doorway, I see the open door as an invitation. Maybe I could step inside, run my hands over the multi-coloured buttons, pull a lever and lift off.

The first kennel I enter belongs to Casanova, a Saint Bernard with a reputation for being affectionate. As soon as I step inside, Casanova jumps – his paws landing heavily on my chest, mouth open, dog breath wafting into my nostrils. I squeeze my eyes shut. *Sluu–urp!* Warm wetness covers my face. I hear Dominic shooing him away and open my eyes. Dominic is looking at me, concerned.

"Leona, are you all right?" he asks.

I look at Casanova wagging his tail beside Dominic and realize that the stupid mutt has just slobbered all over me.

"That is the most disgusting—" I start.

Dominic starts laughing. "Sorry, it's just you should see your face," he says, trying to control himself.

I have this sudden urge to lick *his* face. See how he likes it.

Dominic lifts the bottom of his T-shirt to wipe my face. His stomach is smooth and hard. "He's just showing you he likes you," he says. "I don't blame him."

He's close enough to kiss. I wonder whether he's just being friendly or if he really does like me. I think of Dara – the cat that nobody wants because she's imperfect.

I step back.

We move on to stick-throwing. I lob one across the yard, and Arnie, a Chihuahua, runs yapping after it. According to Clive, Arnie is what Arnold Schwarzenegger would look like if he didn't take steroids.

"I don't get it. Why do dogs get so excited about fetching sticks?" I say.

"Maybe we like throwing sticks, and really they're entertaining us," says Dominic.

Dominic, I realize, has a really weird way of

looking at things. Arnie returns, drops the stick at my feet and looks up at me with his big brown eyes. The stick is wet. Dominic picks it up and throws it lazily. It doesn't go as far as mine.

"Isn't there something you'd rather be doing than throwing sticks?" I ask.

Dominic's eyes are thoughtful, mysterious. "It's not that simple. You can't just do what you want," he says.

"Yeah, but you can try. I mean, I want to be a vet. No one I know has even done their A levels, let alone set foot in a university, and the careers woman at school said I was being overambitious. To top it off, I'm scared of dogs."

"Not any more," Dominic says.

I look at the Staffie, who's chewing a deflated rugby ball in his kennel. It was kept as a fighting dog and now Clive's teaching it to behave, but I still don't trust it.

"Why are you scared of dogs?" Dominic asks.

A memory flashes through my mind. People yell, my dad laughs, my little fingers reach out to pet a doggie, my back thuds to the ground, pain burns my stomach, screams...

"Just am," I reply.

The next day I realize I'm humming along to that awful "Desert Rose" song that is playing on the radio in reception. There must be something in the air, because all the animals are acting a little weird too. Roger is gnawing at his cage as if planning an escape, and Dara buries herself under the blankets of her bed when I try to play with her. Only the tortoise, his head still inside his shell, is the same as always. He's been eating the lettuce we leave for him, though, so he must be coming out occasionally.

Dominic and I take Einstein the Dalmatian for a walk in the park. It's so hot today; it's unbearable. We move like snails through the park. Bodies, like beached whales, lie about, turning red in the sun. Even Einstein doesn't want to walk. I've been watching Einstein carefully, but I can't figure out how he earned his name. He goes over to the shade of a willow tree, turns around three times, as if checking his tail is still attached, and then sits down.

The storm comes out of the blue. First there's a breeze, then a wind, and a huge black and purple cloud rumbles across the sky, casting a shadow. At first we just stand and watch it, as if we're watching a film. Einstein barks at it. Like that's going to help. But when the first drops of rain begin to fall, Dominic grabs my hand and the three of us run back to the sanctuary.

Dominic and I push through the doors, and Einstein circles us, wrapping his lead around our legs. I stumble, taking Dominic with me. He puts his arm against the wall, so he won't crash into me. Our bodies touch. His black eyes glitter. His lips, soft and warm, meet mine. Rain drums the roof and windows, water gushes outside, cats meow, dogs bark, a gate bangs in the wind. It rains and rains and rains, and we kiss and kiss and kiss. Einstein is silent. Maybe he's not such a stupid dog after all.

♥ ♥ ♥

I know as soon as I see Mum put the phone down and give me a guilty look.

"We're just talking, that's all. I owe him that," she says – but I don't believe her. This is how it starts. She comes towards me, but I shrug her off and go to my room. Music drifts in through the window. *"You're my desert rain…"*

I slam the window shut and hurl one of the little animal ornaments I've been collecting against the wall. It smashes. I do the same to another, then another. Mum calls, "Leona, are you all right?" from the other side of the door. I ignore her. I'm furious at her, at him, and most of all, at myself, for believing that this time would be different. For becoming a fool myself. I crawl into bed and bury myself under the blankets like Dara did earlier.

I must fall asleep, because when I open my eyes, it's morning. I avoid Mum and leave the flat. It is cool and damp. Everything looks grey, even the spaceship.

Dominic comes up to me when I'm cleaning Roger's cage.

"Hey," he says, smiling.

I continue cleaning. He brushes the hair from my face.

"So, you wanna go and see *Starburst*? It's about a gamma-ray explosion that threatens to destroy the planet."

"Sounds rubbish," I say.

"Oh. I thought it was your kind of thing."

"I'm not in the habit of going to the cinema with criminals."

He is silent.

"I mean, you could be a con artist, a thief, a serial killer," I continue.

"They don't give you community service if you're serial killer," he says.

"What is it, then? What did you do?"

For the first time, his eyes are troubled. I'm scared of what he's going to tell me about who he is.

"Forget it," I say, and storm off, leaving the cage open. I hope Roger doesn't escape.

♥ ♥ ♥

Mum tries to speak to me when I get home.

"I'm not in the mood," I say.

"Leona, it's just … I'm not like you. I can't just... Look, you're going off to college or whatever. Your dad is the only thing I know."

I ignore her, but I have a feeling that we're more alike than she thinks. We're both cowards; we both stick to what we know.

On my way to the sanctuary the next day, I stop in shock – the spaceship has disappeared. The council must have painted over it.

I look for Dominic everywhere, but I can't find him. Finally, I track Faith down and ask her where he is.

"Oh, I'm not entirely... I was expecting … but on the other hand…"

Typical. She's clueless as usual.

"But isn't he meant to be doing community service?"

"Oh, that was only for two weeks. He stayed on

longer, probably … well, you two seemed to be…"

I guess she's not that clueless after all.

Two weeks' community service… What did he get done for? Stealing some pic 'n' mix? It doesn't matter anyway. I've blown it.

On the walk home, I try to ignore the blank wall where the spaceship used to be.

A few days later I find myself gaping at the wall again. The blank space has been replaced by a girl. A beautiful girl, striding forward, one foot in front of the other, red hair flowing behind her, as if she's crashing through the wall. Her amber eyes are fierce. Half-girl, half-cat. No. Half-girl, half-lioness. A colourful medley of creatures follows in her wake – an old rat, a one-eyed kitten, a tortoise with a cracked shell… The pieces of the puzzle fall into place. It's a message from Dominic. He's WallBreaker. He was prosecuted for graffiti and he's done it again. The girl on the wall is me!

♥ ♥ ♥

The sanctuary is in chaos. Faith has gone into labour. Debbie has taken her to the hospital and Clive is on one of his fishing trips, leaving me as the only full-time volunteer on duty. There's loads of cleaning and feeding and organizing to do. The phone rings constantly.

I leave the dogs till last, then go into each kennel as quickly as I can to give them their food – until only one remains. The Staffie. As I approach, I pray that Clive has named him Gandhi or something equally reassuring. He barks as I approach. The name on his kennel reads "Muhammad Ali".

I take a deep breath and think of the Leona on the wall. Leona, fierce and brave, striding through all obstacles. I walk slowly, calmly, towards the kennel, even though I feel wobbly inside. I look at the dog's yellow eyes – and realize that Ali is just like me. He's scared of people getting too close. He jumps up at the fence, growling. I don't flinch. I stand still by the gate until he stops barking and moves away. I unlock the bolt, open the gate and go inside. Then I top up his food and water as if it's no big deal and leave, closing the gate behind me.

Debbie returns soon after, gushing about Aphrodisia – which is what Faith has decided to call her baby girl. The poor child will be bullied to death.

I pass the terrarium on the way Faith's office to look for Dominic's address and see the tortoise's little bald head moving back and forth as he attacks the apple in front of him.

He lives in one of the high rises on Orchard Estate. A stupid name really because there isn't a tree in sight.

A little boy opens the door. He's got the same mad hair as Dominic.

"Is Dominic in?" I ask.

He shakes his head.

"Do you know where he is?"

He points upwards.

"In the flat above?" I ask.

He sighs, as if he's dealing with a prize idiot,

and walks towards the stairwell, leaving the door open behind him. We go up to the very top floor, then walk along the balcony that leads round to the other side of the building, where a ladder is leaning against the wall. It's old and paint-splattered and very long. The boy skips off.

I climb the ladder one step at a time. I don't look down.

Dominic is on his hands and knees at the far end of the roof. Spray cans, pens and bits of cardboard are littered all over the place. As I get closer, I see that he's cutting a stencil out of a huge bit of cardboard with a carpet knife. My shadow falls over him. He looks up, surprised. His smooth brown skin glows in the evening sun. I move closer. I think about how he exposed himself by doing that graffiti up the side of the bookies. Slowly, I lift my T-shirt.

He doesn't recoil from the pink and shiny scars on my stomach, but reaches out and runs his fingertips along them.

"What happened?" he says.

I tell him about my dad, who used to organize dog fights when I was little, and how I was attacked by a pit bull. I tell him about how he hits my mum sometimes or, more often than not, shacks up with another woman or just goes off on a caper – and how she keeps taking him back.

Dominic listens, then plants a kiss on my stomach, making it flutter. Then he stands up and kisses me on the collarbone, then on my lips.

The sunset is a deep red, which is a sign of pollution – but it looks wicked.

"I think I know what to name the tortoise," he says.

"What?"

"Red."

We hold hands and look out over the antennas, the rooftops, the cars and trucks zooming along overpasses, the buses going round roundabouts, the factories in the distance pumping out plumes of smoke, the skyscrapers in the city beyond, and for the first time, I don't see the world ending, but the future, unfurling before me.

Just a Friend

Dyan Sheldon

"I should dump Simon. I know I should. He's way more trouble than he's worth." Molly flops down on the sofa, a cola in her hand and an unhappy look on her face. "More trouble than anybody's worth."

"Don't tell me. Let me guess," says Schuyler. "You and Simon had a fight." He slaps his forehead. Mock-dramatically. "What's next? Flying cows? Raining rabbits?"

"Ha ha ha." Molly kicks off her shoes. "That *is* what you think, though, isn't it, Sky? You think I should dump him."

In the middle of the ocean would be nice.

"I never said you should break up with him,"

says Schuyler. Not that he hasn't had plenty of opportunity to say that – or something similar. He hears all about it whenever Molly and Simon have a fight. And, since their relationship is like a war that is occasionally interrupted by periods of peace, he hears about it a lot. But it's none of his business, not really. He listens, but he doesn't want to interfere. He doesn't think he should.

Schuyler sets the snacks on the coffee table and sits down beside her. "It's up to you, Mol. It's your life."

Molly groans. "But everybody must think I'm nuts, right? Putting up with him and all his crap."

Barking mad. Certifiable. Ought to be locked away for your own good.

"I think you're the only person he annoys so much." Schuyler picks up the remote. "Everybody else likes Simon well enough."

Even Schuyler would probably like Simon if it weren't for Molly. Not love him, not want to be stuck in a lift with him for more than two minutes or give him a kidney, but not want him stranded in the middle of the Atlantic, trying to drink seawater and fish with his hands. "He may grow up to be a serial killer or a hedge fund manager or a politician or something else pretty reprehensible, but right now he's just a regular bloke. You know, he's OK."

"So you want to know what he did this time?"

Schuyler has noticed that a lot of girls look like deformed potatoes when they scowl, but Molly still looks pretty.

"He broke our date so he can watch football with his mates."

It's obviously Simon who is out of his mind. Schuyler wouldn't break a date with Molly if he had appendicitis. He'd rather die in her arms. Even if they were in the town centre when it happened and pigeons were pecking at spilled chips and half-eaten burgers all around him and shoppers were taking pictures on their phones.

"But that's what guys do. It's a big game." Schuyler only knows this second-hand. He's never watched a game in his life.

"And what am I, Pot Noodles?" Molly scoops

up a handful of peanuts. "And anyway, it's Saturday night. Saturday night is date night."

Not for everyone.

"Oh, hey." A new thought makes Molly's eyes widen, so they look even bluer. "You didn't change your plans to hold my hand, did you?"

"Nothing important." The band can practise another night. They're playing Lucy Furimsky's party at the end of the month, not The O2. Schuyler waves the remote at Molly. "I'd rather have double-bill cheesy sci-fi night."

Molly leans against him the way a cat would – scattering peanuts on him and the sofa the way a cat wouldn't. "Simon always lets me down, but not you. You're always there for me."

Both these statements are true. Something's always coming up at the last minute for Simon. Or he forgets he's seeing Molly and makes other plans. Or he strains something playing football or climbing up a wall or jumping between buildings. Or he and Molly have a fight. And Schuyler always steps in. He's always drawn the line at shopping, though – no way is he going shopping with her; that's what her girlfriends are for – but he's there to walk around graveyards in the rain taking photos for an art project, or to break into her flat when her parents are away and she locks herself out, or to help blow up sixty balloons for her grandmother's birthday. Or to lend a shoulder to cry on. Good old Schuyler, faithful and loyal. He was probably a dog in his previous life.

She squeezes his arm. "What would I do if you weren't my best friend?"

Schuyler presses the power button. "I reckon you'd have to marry me."

Molly laughs.

After Molly goes home, Schuyler stares at himself in the bathroom mirror for a lot longer than boys who look like a bird made human usually do. The medley of songs he thinks of as the soundtrack to his life plays in his head. Ray Charles ... Roy Orbison ... Linda Ronstadt ... Billie Holiday ... The Everly Brothers ... Conway Twitty ... Charlie Patton...

It's a long list. There is no shortage of songs about unrequited love.

"What's wrong with you?" he asks his reflection.

As if he doesn't know.

Schuyler's had a thing for Molly from day one. The first time he saw her she was sitting by the window in their tutor group. She smiled (not at him); Schuyler walked into a desk. Meeting Molly was like being struck by lightning, only without being killed. Silent, eternal suffering instead of instantaneous death.

Besides his tutor group, she was in his science class and his English class that year. So it should have been easy to get to know her. Only Molly is smart and funny and outgoing and one of the prettiest girls in their year, and Schuyler is a serious brainbox and shy and looks like a geek. He could never get up the nerve to talk to her. Until that class trip to the theatre when fate decided to help him out.

At the end of the play, everyone else in their group left by one set of stairs and he and Molly left by another. They came out onto an unfamiliar street and Schuyler sat down on the kerb. Molly wanted to know what he was doing. The others had to be just around the corner. Schuyler said that losing two students had to be the most exciting thing that had happened to any of them all day and he didn't want to spoil anybody's fun. Molly thought that was hilarious. She said she didn't know he had such a wicked sense of humour.

They sat together going back on the bus. It turned out they both liked old music, and really bad old B-movies, and the Hitchhiker's Guide books, and about a billion other things. They talked all the way home.

He could have asked her out dozens of times. He even came close once or twice. Like that time they got caught in the thunderstorm. He put his jacket over both of them and they huddled against a wall. He could feel her breath on his cheek. She was as close to him as skin; so close he was sure she must be able to hear his heart pounding. *Do something*, he told himself. *Kiss her.* She was looking at him as if maybe he was going to kiss her – as if maybe she might even kiss him back. But he didn't, and the moment passed. Just like all the other moments.

And then they were best friends, and he didn't say anything because he didn't want to risk losing her completely. In case, after he told her how he felt, she threw up, or ran away shaking and screaming with tears streaming down her face. In case she would never say so much as "Hi" to him again. Never. Not even if it would end world hunger.

And then along came Simon. He wasn't the first boy Molly ever went out with, but he was the first who got the words "boy" and "friend" put together.

Schuyler can't stop the thought: *It should've been me.*

He blows out a fist of air. "This is it," he tells his reflection. Sternly. "I'm giving you an ultimatum. You either say something to Molly, or you stop thinking about her like that. There are plenty of other girls around. Ask one of them out."

His reflection gives him the finger.

He doesn't want to go out with anyone else.

♥ ♥ ♥

Schuyler is standing a metre or so from the women's changing room, trying to look interested in the racks of something called "leisurewear", though he would call them pyjamas. Schuyler is waiting for Molly, who is looking for a "frock that rocks" for the Valentine's Day dance. This is shop number four. Molly says that all the frocks she's tried on so far haven't rocked; they've just hung there and wobbled. Schuyler shifts uncomfortably. There are no other blokes in this part of the store. Just Schuyler, holding Molly's handbag in his arms like a sleeping pig. He wishes he'd worn a suit. If he'd worn a suit people might think he's a bodyguard. And not a nerd.

So far, the ultimatum hasn't worked. Not only has he still not said anything to her, but when she asked him to come shopping with her because Sylvia, her other best friend, has been grounded for the next two hundred years, he didn't say no. *No, Molly, you have got to be out of your tiny mind. Men don't like shopping; they'd rather be in combat.* He hummed and hawed, but he couldn't quite get the "N" word out. She begged. She said she knew it was a lot to ask but this was important. She's really excited about the dance and she couldn't find the right dress without some help.

"It's the first Valentine's Day I've actually had a real boyfriend." Needless to say, she didn't dump Simon. "Me! How historic is that?"

"World War Two pales into insignificance beside it," said Schuyler.

"Don't be so cynical; it's romantic. It's the first time anything romantic's happened to me. Maybe you're not into romance, but I think it rules."

"So does that mean I don't have to send you a secret admirer card this year?"

She laughed. "I should've known that was you!"

But she hadn't.

Schuyler rocks on his heels. How many dresses did she take in with her? He's been standing here a long time. A couple of the saleswomen are giving him curious looks. They think he's been standing here a long time too. Maybe they think he's

some kind of pervert for hanging around ladies'
leisurewear holding an overstuffed bright red tar-
tan handbag with a string of charms and beads
wrapped around the handle. He's just about to text
Molly to see if she went out the wrong door and
ended up in the Megabrantis Cluster, when she
suddenly appears in the entrance to the changing
room. Looking like she wants to break his heart.

"Sorry," she says, "but I had to try on everything
like three times. What do you think about this?"

"It's swell." Too good for Simon Kendrick.
"You look really gor— really good."

"What about my bum?" She turns slowly
round. "Is my bum OK?"

"It looks OK to me. You haven't grown a tail
or anything."

"You think Simon will like it?"

"He'll love it." *Unless there's more wrong with
him than I think.*

She holds out the skirt. "You swear I look
all right?"

She looks like a butterfly. One of those exotic

butterflies that are more a work of art than an insect.

"Yes."

"Brilliant!" Molly turns back towards the changing room. "Now we can look for shoes."

"This time I mean it," sobs Molly. "No way am I ever going to have anything to do with Simon Kendrick again. Not even if the earth's hit by an asteroid and we're the last two people left alive."

Schuyler slaps the side of his head as though trying to clear it. "I'm having the weirdest sensation, Mol. Almost like I've heard this all before."

Only Molly's not in a laughing mood right now. "You have heard it before. But you'll never hear it again. I swear on the grave of Boudicca; this is it. I don't care if he crawls over broken glass to apologize; this time we're through. Finished. Dead as the dinosaurs."

Schuyler holds out the box of tissues. Her eye make-up has run so much she looks like a raccoon. A very pretty raccoon wearing dangling earrings, but a raccoon nonetheless. "You're upset. When you calm dow—"

"No, I really mean it, Schuyler. Simon Kendrick is now officially dumped. The only word I want to hear from him is 'goodbye'."

They've had a fight. Again. Simon went into nuclear meltdown because she was talking to another boy.

"Talking?" says Schuyler. "You talk to me all the time."

But Simon's not jealous of Schuyler. He is, however, jealous of Lucas Adamani. Lucas Adamani doesn't look like a pelican. Wearing glasses.

A bunch of them were hanging out at Starbucks, and Molly wound up next to Lucas. Simon claims she ignored him completely. Simon says she was flirting with Lucas.

"Flirting!" wails Molly. "Gar! I wasn't flirting. I was just chatting. And I have known Lucas longer than I've known Simon. I have talked to him before."

Simon said if she liked talking to Lucas so

much she could go to the flippin' Valentine's dance with him.

Molly reminded him that Lucas has a girlfriend.

"And you used to have a boyfriend," said Simon.

Schuyler's almost afraid to ask. "So...?"

The dance is only two days away.

"So I'm not going, am I?" Fresh tears fill her eyes. "I wish I'd never met him. I wish he'd be abducted by aliens. Why do I always fall for such hooples?"

Simon manages not to say, "Don't ask me."

"Some romantic evening," mumbles Molly. "Sitting at home by myself."

"There's no need for that," says Schuyler. "You've still got me."

Schuyler's new motto is "Do or die." Molly thinks he's sarcastic and cynical and as romantic as boiled cabbage? Well, he'll show her she's wrong.

She wants romance; she's going to get romance. Instead of one of their cheesy sci-fi nights watching an old black and white film featuring an alien monster wearing shoes, or a cardboard spaceship that shakes when someone walks near it, they're having the Alternative Valentine's Day dance. Fate's decided to join Schuyler's team again: his parents are away for the night so he doesn't have to explain what he's doing to them. He asked his mother to name three really romantic movies, and he got all three. He's lugged the fairy lights out of the loft and strung them all over the living room. He's bought enough candles to torch Rome, and burnt himself lighting them. He's got those corn nut things Molly likes, and olives instead of boring old peanuts and crisps. He's rehearsed what he's going to say so much, you'd think he were addressing the United Nations. He's cut himself shaving, changed his shirt three times and got a song ready to play that will tell her everything she needs to know even before he opens his mouth: Ray Charles singing the classic "You Don't Know Me", about someone who's always been just a friend to the person he loves.

By seven, when Molly should be turning the

corner at the end of the road, Schuyler's so nervous he thinks he may be having a stroke. He turns on the stereo when he hears the bell, and takes several deep breaths. He wipes his hands on his jeans and takes a few more breaths. There's another ring.

Damn. There aren't any lights on in the front room. What if she thinks he's forgotten the way Simon always did and isn't home? He rushes to the hall, and trips over the cat. He'll be lucky not to kill himself before he gets to the door.

As soon as he opens it, he wishes he had.

Molly's talking on her phone, but that isn't really what he notices. What hits him like a very large truck is that she's dressed up: rocking frock, new shoes and her good coat, not the jacket she wears every day.

She's going to the dance.

Schuyler steps forward to block her view into the house.

"Bye-bye," she says in a voice she never uses with him. "See you soon." She snaps the phone shut and looks at him. "Schuyler!"

"You didn't have to dress up for me," says Schuyler. He hopes she doesn't realize he's wearing his good-luck shirt, the one he only wears for gigs.

"Oh, Schuyler..." Molly makes a sad, apologetic face. "I'm really sorry. I tried to ring you before, but you didn't answer."

"So you and Simon made up?" If Schuyler holds onto the door frame any more tightly he'll break it.

"Yeah. You know..." She shrugs. As if it's something that's happened to her, like getting a cold. "It looks like it."

"Right." He takes a small step back, already starting to shut the door. "Well, you don't want to keep him waiting. Have a swell time. I'll see you—"

She's peering under his arm. "Why is it so dark in there? What's with all those fairy lights?"

"You've seen fairy lights before." Why didn't he shut the living-room door?

"Not in February. It looks like Christmas in there."

Could be; it's definitely snowing in his heart.

"No, it's only—"

"What is that?" Her nose is twitching. "Do I smell jasmine?" Twitch-twitch. "Sandalwood? Patchouli?"

"It's just some scented candles."

"Candles?" And suddenly she pushes past him into the hall. "Oh my God." Molly stares into the living room, listening. "Is that Ray Charles?" She recognizes the song. She moves her stare from the living room to him. She looks as if she's not sure who he is. But she's thinking about it.

"What is all this, Sky? What's going on?" But he can tell from her expression that she has a pretty good idea.

Say it, Schuyler tells himself. *This is your chance. Tell her the truth. I'm crazy about you. I think about you all the time. Open your arms.*

Ask her to dance…

Into the silence, the phone Molly's still holding starts to ring.

My First
Kiss

Sarah Webb

First day back. Last class. English. I know something's going on behind me but I don't turn round. It's probably Nessa Winkleman slagging me off again for sitting up the front and being teacher's pet. Nessa's a wagon of the highest order. Unfortunately she's also the most popular girl in our year. Go figure.

When our teacher, Miss Carmichael, walks into the room, all curves and curls, she smiles warmly at me. Disaster. I know she means well but I wish she wouldn't single me out. She doesn't get that I just want to lurk under the radar like everyone else (except for Nessa, who has to be the centre of attention). I want to be anonymous. Normal.

Miss Carmichael stands at the front of the room and looks at us, blinking a few times. She seems nervous. "Welcome back, everyone," she says. "I guess we'll get straight to it." She picks up a pen and writes "Functional Writing" on the whiteboard. "Can anyone tell me what functional writing is?"

I don't put up my hand. I look around. No one else does either. Then I accidentally catch Miss Carmichael's eye again. Big mistake.

"I bet you know, don't you, Clara?" she asks.

I shake my head and stare down at my table-top. When I look up once more, her right eye is twitching a little at the corner, like it always does when she's stressed, although it doesn't usually happen until towards the end of class.

"When was the last time any of you lot wrote a proper letter?" she says.

I look around again. Blank faces. I look back at Miss Carmichael.

She tilts her head. "How about you, Clara?"

Can't the woman leave me alone? OK, I know

she gives me books to bring home, novels mainly, and books on creative writing – we don't have a school library and the library in town is small – and I know they're her own books, not the school's, cos her name's written in small, neat handwriting inside the front cover, Beth Carmichael; and I do appreciate it, but that doesn't give her the right to pick on me in class.

Something hits the back of my head. I rub my hair and a ball of chewed-up paper drops to the floor. Disgusting! I swing round. Nessa gazes back at me innocently.

"What, Clawa?" she mouths, purposely mis-pronouncing my name. Then she turns to Miss Carmichael. "Seriously, miss, *letters*? Can't we do something a bit more exciting? Come on, no one writes letters any more." She fiddles with the collar of her shirt, making sure it's sticking up the required "cool" amount, and then flicks her poker-straight bleached hair back over her shoulders.

Miss Carmichael is clutching the whiteboard

pen so hard her knuckles have turned white. Her chest is heaving up and down under her tight red polo neck and her cheeks are flushed. I don't think she's cut out for teaching. And having Nessa in the class can't make things easy.

"No, Nessa, we can't," she says finally, her voice only wobbling a little bit. "We're doing letter writing and that's final. You'll all be writing to students at a school in Toronto called St Xavier's. Toronto's the largest city in Canada for anyone who's not hot on geography." She looks at pointedly Nessa.

I perk up a little. Toronto. That sounds interesting. But from the bored expressions around me, I can tell no one else agrees.

Miss Carmichael continues. "You're going to write a letter in longhand for homework. At least half an A4 page, please, and we'll check them over in class tomorrow for layout and spelling. Then I'll post them all, and hopefully in about two weeks you'll get a letter back from your pen pal in Toronto. Those of you who would like to continue writing to their new friends after that can. But the first letter is compulsory."

Nessa is waving her hand around in the air. "What are we supposed to say?"

"Just tell them about your life," Miss Carmichael says. "The kind of clothes and music you like, that sort of thing. It will be a wonderful cultural exchange."

"Hang on" – Nessa's eyes brighten and she sits up a little – "are there any boys at this St Xavier's place, miss?"

"It is a mixed school, yes, but I've asked for girls."

Nessa groans, but I for one am hugely relieved. I wouldn't have a clue what to say to a boy. They're like an alien species to me. And no normal boy in his right mind would be interested in me, and that's a fact.

Miss Carmichael hands out sheets of paper with the Canadian students' names on them. Mine says Alex Goodman.

♥ ♥ ♥

Summer Cottage
Haven
West Cork
Ireland
Monday, 3 September

Dear Alex,
How are you? What's the weather like in
Canada?

I stop writing and wince. Did I really just ask my
new pen pal about the weather? How pathetic. I
try again.

Dear Alex,
I hope this finds you well.

That's even worse! Now I sound like an old granny.

Dear Alex,
I'm Clara McCarthy and I live in Haven, a village
in West Cork, which is in the south of Ireland.

I doubt if you've heard of Haven; it's pretty tiny! What's Toronto like? It's the biggest city in Canada, right? I look forward to hearing all about it. I think this letter-writing cultural exchange thing is pretty cool. Most of the girls in my class think it's "like, lame-o" and "seriously sad" but they're complete eejits (that's Irish for dorks!). You have to imagine them flicking their hair back and adjusting the collars of their shirts when they say this (in a fake American accent – they think it's cool to sound American).

I'm thirteen and I'm in second year at St Belinda's College in Skibbereen. It's about five miles from my house. I live with my mum, Olga. She works part-time as a teaching assistant in the local primary school. She's pretty OK for a mum. Our teacher, Miss Carmichael, said we should tell you about the kind of things we're into, so here goes: I like reading (a lot!), writing (I'm writing a book about a girl and her guardian angel at the moment but I've only done three chapters), taking photographs of the sea and nature and stuff. I like music with a strong beat, rock mainly. And I also like pizza: does that count as something I'm into? ☺

That's about it, really. How about you?

I've enclosed some photos of where I live – Haven village, our house, and the lough (lake) near us, Lough Hyne. It's a saltwater lake, which is pretty unusual. Mum's really into kayaking so we do that a lot on the lough in the summer. Anyway, hope you like the photos.

Yours sincerely,
Clara McCarthy

212 Stanford Mills
Richmond Hill
Ontario
Canada
Friday, September 14

Dear Clara,
Thanks for your letter. I'm really into proper

letters. I know it's old-fashioned and everything, but I think letters are really cool. Like a bite of history. No one ever keeps emails in a shoebox for years, right?

I'm totally psyched to have an Irish pen pal. My mom's from Ireland, a place called Kerry. She's always talking about growing up there and it sounds awesome. She met Dad at the hospital in Toronto where they both work. She's a doctor; he's a pharmacist. It was love at first prescription apparently. You call them prescriptions in Ireland, right, not scripts?

So what am I into? Pizza, too, I guess! And, like you, I read a lot. I love books by Irish authors like James Joyce; he's really cool. I write poems sometimes and short stories, but I'm impressed that you're writing a whole book – how awesome is that?!

I'm kind of interested in being a surgeon some day, but don't tell Mom that – she'd freak out. She's always saying medicine is a mug's game; bad conditions, lousy pay, ridiculous hours, yadda yadda

yadda, but she doesn't mean it. I know she gets a big kick from her job. She works at SickKids (short for Hospital for Sick Children, but no one calls it that) – she's a consultant paediatric oncologist (thank God for spell check, right?!) and she's always talking about "her" kids.

I also play a lot of hockey. Music-wise I like U2 – they're Irish, right? My mom got me into them and they rock. I also like the Chili Peppers.

My school is OK, I guess. Oh, and my teacher's Irish – Mrs Jackson, she's from Cork originally. You Paddies sure get around! You asked about Toronto... Well, I live in Richmond Hill, which is about twelve miles from downtown Toronto, with my mom and dad. Toronto's pretty big – two and a half million people – and it's on this lake called Lake Ontario. It's starting to get cold here and the winters are freezing, but not as cold as in the north; it gets insanely cold up there. Sorry, talking about the weather – how 'ime is that?!

Can't think of anything else to say right now. Do you know anything about Kerry? Have you any

photos of it? You're an amazing photographer by
the way. And that lake really is something! The
photo of the mossy trees hanging over the water
is my favourite. Those trees have such character
– they look like little old ladies, all stooped over and
everything. You've got one hell of a talent, Clara!

Best wishes,

Alex

PS Sorry for blabbing on so much. As I
said, I like writing and I get a bit carried away
sometimes. Mrs Jackson said some of you might
like to write on a regular basis, like proper pen
pals. Are you up for it? I sure am! What do you
think? I hope you write back and say yes!!!

Haven

Ireland

Thursday, 27 September

Dear Alex,

Thanks for your letter. I'd love to be pen pals.

And I agree, there's something really special about proper letters, especially ones that have flown the whole way over the Atlantic. And you weren't blabbing on at all. I really liked hearing about your mum and her job and everything. It must be amazing, being able to help people like that, especially kids.

My dad's from Kerry too, a place called Dingle. It's famous for its dolphin, Fungi. Not that I see him all that much. Dad, I mean, not Fungi! He and Mum split up when I was three. Sorry, I don't know why I just told you that. Anyway, Kerry's lovely. I'll print some photos out for you.

You said you live with your mum and dad; I'm an only child too. There's just me and Mum and we're pretty close. I don't know what I'd do without her. I feel like I can tell her anything, like when this girl at school, Nessa, started calling me names and basically being a real bitch. I told Mum about it and she went ballistic, threatened to sue the school and everything.

I was offered a place in a boarding school in Dublin last year and Mum wanted me to take it, but I couldn't leave her on her own like that. It wouldn't be fair. Not after everything she's done for me. Besides, I'd miss her too much. I hope I'm not boring you with all this personal stuff. Sometimes it's easier to write things down, you know.

I hate school. I try really hard but I'm really behind. I know I'm not thick or anything, it's just the way some of the teachers teach doesn't suit me and it's hard to keep up. I'm pretty good at English though. Mum says it's cos I read so much.

Speaking of books, what else do you like to read? I like all kinds of things – paranormal romance, books about angels, real-life stories – but my favourite writer is John Green I LOVE John Green! He's American, right?

That's it for now.

Bye,

Clara XXX

♥ ♥ ♥

Ontario
Canada
Wednesday, October 24

Hey Clara,

Thanks for your letter and the photos of Kerry.
It looks like a really beautiful place. Mom's always
saying she's gotta go back for a visit and I can
see why. I Googled that dolphin, Fungi. He's a big
star, on YouTube and everything. Sorry you don't
get to see your dad much. Loads of my friends'
folks are divorced and I know it sucks. But I guess
it's better than hearing them argue all the time,
right? Anyway, your mom sounds nice and I like
hearing about your life and everything, so don't
worry about that at all.

I'm sorry to hear about school too, and
Nessa. I used to get kicked around by this kid in
middle school, so I know what that's like, believe
me. I was kind of short for my age, but I've
caught up. I'm one of the tallest in the class now.

I wasn't always an only child. I had a little sister, Becca, but she died last fall. She was out on her scooter one day, and this car swerved to avoid a dog and skidded onto the sidewalk and hit her. Mom still can't talk about it much; it really cut her up. Sometimes I'll go into her study, late, and she's just sitting there, staring at the screen, like a zombie. But she's a lot better than she used to be. Whoa, serious stuff! Sorry about that. I know what you mean about writing being easier than talking — it feels good to be able to tell you things, you know, personal stuff.

And I can't believe you like John Green. Me, too! <u>Will Grayson, Will Grayson</u> is one of the funniest things I've ever read! We have so much in common, Clara, seriously — it's spooky! And I have something to tell you. I was lying about reading Joyce, trying to big myself up. Sorry! I did try reading <u>Ulysses</u> once but it was too freaking weird. I'm not much into books about vampires or angels, I have to tell you. Movie-wise, I'm crazy about classic sci-fi stuff like <u>The Matrix</u> and

<u>Star Wars</u>. Man, are they good to watch! I've seen them all hundreds of times!

OK, better motor, hockey practice tonight.

Later, Alex X

Haven

Ireland

Thursday, 1 November

Dear Alex,

I was so sorry to read about Becca. That's really tragic. I can understand why your mum was (and still is) devastated. I can't imagine what it must be like to lose a little sister or a daughter.

I had a really crap day in school today and reading your letter helped me realize that there are worse things than stupid girls saying stupid things. I hope you don't mind if I get it off my chest, though. Nessa Winkleman is such a cow. Sometimes I pronounce words wrong and she teases me about it, saying them back to me in a horrible mouthy way, like I'm slow. I can't tell Mum about it, cos she'll freak out and storm into the school again and threaten the head; and it didn't do any good the last time she did that. Nessa stopped picking on me for a while, but then she just started up again. I try to ignore her, but she stands right in my face, or throws things at me. It's starting to really get to me. And I have five more years of her to put up with – help!

I'm too tired to write any more, I'm afraid. I haven't been sleeping very well and I'm wrecked.

Write soon. Your letters make my days a lot brighter (sorry, that sounds a bit hippy-dippy, I know!). And telling you my problems really helps. I feel like I can tell you anything. You like REAL things, like books and movies and writing, not like the girls in my school who are complete airheads and are only interested in boys and clothes. It's pathetic. There's more to life than having a boyfriend and the right skinny jeans!

Don't get me wrong, I like boys and everything, but I'm not completely obsessed like they are.

Thanks for being there,

Clara XXX

PS I love the _Star Wars_ films too. I used to watch them with my dad every weekend – he's a huge fan. _The Empire Strikes Back_ is my favourite. Gotta love Yoda! "Meditate on this I will"

PPS I meant to ask – are you on Facebook? We should hook up. Our Internet's been down for the last few weeks, which is a real pain, but Mum's getting it fixed tomorrow.

PPPS I've enclosed the first chapter of my book, _Broken Wings_. Please tell me if you think it's awful. I'd really appreciate your honest opinion.

I feel a zing of excitement. The Internet is finally working again and I'm dying to find Alex on Facebook. I don't know why I didn't suggest it before. We've been writing letters and emails to each other for two months now. I know it sounds crazy, but it already feels like we're old friends. I don't really have any close friends, so it means a lot to me and I'm dying to see some photos of her.

I wolf down my breakfast, then park myself in front of the computer and click straight into Facebook. I type "Alex Goodman, Canada" into the search bar, and a second later five faces stare back at me from their small profile boxes. But they're all boys. I try again. This time I type "Alex Goodman, Toronto". Two faces: a white-haired man, and a boy of about my age or a little older with a mop of dark curly brown hair, bright blue eyes and a lopsided smile. That can't be right. Out of curiosity, I check the younger Alex's info.

School	St Xavier's College
Music	U2, Red Hot Chili Peppers
Sport	Ice hockey

St Xavier's ... U2 ... Chili Peppers ... *ice* hockey! I start to feel a little faint. It all fits. Alex is a boy.

A boy! I've been telling all my secrets to a bloody Canadian *boy*. I think back through my letters, feeling physically sick. I've told him everything – all about Nessa, Mum, Dad, even Fungi the dolphin, for God's sake. And I sent him a chapter of my angel romance. Cringe! He must think I'm such an idiot. And that last letter, about how "she" was different from other girls. Oh dear God! How stupid am I? I put my head in my hands. What the hell do I do now?

Ontario
Canada
Saturday, November 24

Dear Clara,
Are you OK? You haven't written for ages and I'm kinda worried about you. Listen, I have news. Mom doesn't want to spend Christmas at home on account of Becca and everything, and her sister, Mona, is always on at her to visit over the

holidays, so this year I think Mom is going to take her up on the offer. We're going to Kerry! That's really near Cork, right?

Have to study now, tests soon, but isn't it awesome? Maybe we can meet up.

Alex X

PS The girls in your class sound totally lame – we have girls like that in our school too! *pulls nasty face*

PPS I'm no angel expert but your chapter rocked. You can really write, Clara! Send me more. I have to find out what happens to Romie and Azeth (great name for a fallen angel, by the way!).

Haven

Ireland

Saturday, 8 December

Dear Alex,

I'm so sorry, but we're going to be away for Christmas. And I'm really behind with my studies, so I'm afraid I'll have to stop writing to you. It's been an amazing cultural experience and I wish you all the best in the future. I hope you enjoy Kerry and Fungi.

Yours,

Clara

December 18

Clara,

WTF? I thought we were friends. Tell me your last letter was a joke. What's going on? I'm freaking out here.

Alex

Miss Carmichael holds me back after class. "Clara, can I have a word with you, please?" she asks.

I can't believe she's doing this. It's the very last class before the Christmas holidays, and I just want to get out of here.

"Clara, the secretary said there was someone in reception looking for you earlier," she says. "An American boy. He said he'd come back after school. Are you expecting anyone?"

Alex! It has to be. What is he doing here? My stomach tenses but then I start to feel angry. This mess is all Miss Carmichael's fault. This whole pen pal thing has been a disaster.

"You lied," I say. "You said they were all girls."

Miss Carmichael looks confused. "Sorry? Who?"

"You know, the pen pals? Mine is called Alex. And he's a boy."

She nods. "He's a really nice boy, brilliant at English just like you, and a big reader."

"You knew?"

She looks a bit sheepish. "I was talking to St Xavier's English teacher and we thought you'd get on well. But what's that got to do with the American boy?"

"Canadian. The boy in reception, I think it's Alex."

"What? What's he doing *here*? And did you tell him everything, Clara? Because I think the secretary may have said something—"

Before she can finish, I'm sprinting out of the classroom, down the corridor and through the main door. I have to get out, get away from all this ... from Alex and Miss Carmichael ... from Nessa ... even Mum. I just want to be alone. But there, standing with his back against the wall in reception, is Alex Goodman in the flesh. And what flesh! His Facebook photo doesn't do him justice. He's gorgeous, and the very last person I want to see.

I stand there, frozen to the spot, staring at him.

He walks towards me. "Clara? I recognize you from your Facebook photo. Clara?" he says again, his gaze gentle and concerned, not angry at all. In an instant I realize that Miss Carmichael was right; the secretary did say something to him. He knows.

"I just want to check you're all right," he continues. "Then I'll leave you alone, I swear. Can you understand me?"

I nod. My eyes well up and I start to cry. My head is spinning. I can't believe he's being so nice. I kept the truth from him and then I shut him out of my life, just stopped writing, even though he sent several letters asking if I was all right, saying he was worried and begging me to write back to him. But I didn't. I ignored him. You see, it felt so good to be normal that I wanted to freeze the two months when I was just Clara McCarthy, no one "special".

Right now I feel completely mortified and humiliated. I drop my head and cover my face with my hands. I want to die. I want to dissolve in my tears and wash away. I've never been so embarrassed in my entire life. I have such a huge lump in my throat that I couldn't speak to him even if I wanted to. Then I feel his hand on my shoulder. It's gentle but firm. I lift my head and look at him.

He starts moving his hands. He's using international sign language. Mum made me learn it a long time ago.

Please don't cry, he signs. *I want to help you.*

That's what friends do.

You can sign? I sign back. *I don't understand. How?*

Becca was deaf. It doesn't matter to me that you are too, Clara. You're still the same person. Is that why you stopped writing to me, because you thought I'd mind? I wouldn't be much of a person if I minded, would I?

Finally I find my voice. "It's not that," I say. "I would have told you eventually. I was just enjoying being normal for a while."

He gives a short laugh. "Normal? You're too smart to be normal, Clara. You have no idea how talented you are. Your photos are something else. And that chapter you sent me was awesome, and I don't even like angel books."

I take a deep breath. "Plus you're a boy," I admit. "I thought I was writing to a girl, and when I found out the truth it freaked me out. I would never have said all that stuff to a boy."

"A girl? Really?" He throws his head back and laughs heartily. "Well, as you can see, I'm not. I'm one hundred per cent male." Then he lifts his eyebrows and smiles at me, a lovely lopsided warm smile, a smile full of promise. My heart practically somersaults out of my chest.

"Can we start again, Clara?" he asks.

I nod and give him a shy smile. "Hi, I'm Clara McCarthy," I say, blushing furiously.

"Alex Goodman, good to meet you." And then he leans towards me and kisses me softly on the cheek. My first kiss.

With thanks to Lorna McCormack from Simply Signing for her invaluable help.

THE
AUTHORS

Katie Dale loves creating characters – both on the page and on-stage. She studied English literature at Sheffield University, followed by a crazy year at drama school, a summer with a national Shakespeare tour and eight months backpacking through South East Asia. Her debut YA novel, *Someone Else's Life*, was a winner of Undiscovered Voices, and she is currently busy on a variety of projects, from novels to picture books, while still occasionally treading the boards as a princess, zombie or fairy when she has time!

Cathy Kelly is an internationally bestselling fiction writer. She lives in Ireland, is married to John, has twin sons called Murray and Dylan (who are ten) and three dogs (who are sisters) called the Puplets of Loveliness, or Dinky, Licky and Scamp. Cathy always wanted to be a writer and went to journalism college after school. She is now a full-time author. She loves reading, watching films, chocolate, lipstick and jeans. This is Cathy's first story for younger readers but she'd like to write more.

Cathy Kelly

Photo by Caroline Briggs

Abby McDonald is the author of eight romantic comedy novels, including *Getting Over Garrett Delaney* and *The Anti-Prom*. Born and raised in Sussex, she recently left the rainy countryside for the blue skies and palm trees of LA. She is twenty-seven years old.

Photo by Ashley Miller

Monica McInerney is the award-winning author of ten bestselling novels for adults, many magazine and newspaper articles and lots of stories written especially for her eighteen nieces and nephews. She grew up in a family of seven children in a small country town in South Australia. For the past twenty-two years, Monica has moved back and forth between Australia and Ireland, her husband's home country. They currently live in Dublin. Fortunately, she loves rainy weather.

Monica McInerney

Sinéad Moriarty is a bestselling author whose work has been published globally. Born and raised in Dublin, Sinéad was inspired by watching her mother, who is an author of children's books, writing at the kitchen table and then being published. From that moment on, her childhood dream was to write a novel. Her first book was *The Baby Trail*. It was published by Penguin and has been translated into twenty-five languages. Her eighth novel, *This Child of Mine*, went straight in at number one in the Irish charts.

Sinéad Moriarty

Joanna Nadin is the bestselling author of the Rachel Riley series for teens, the award-winning Penny Dreadful series for younger readers, and the acclaimed young adult novels *Wonderland* and *Paradise*. A former journalist and special adviser to the prime minister, Joanna also freelances as a speechwriter. She lives in Bath.

jo nadin
x.

Adele Parks was a swotty, sometimes lonely kid who found books were her friends; she specialized in daydreaming and unsuitable crushes. The combination of these skills led her to publish her first novel, *Playing Away*. It was very rude and therefore, not unsurprisingly, very successful. She has since published twelve novels, all of which have been top-ten bestsellers. Her work has been translated into twenty-five languages. Adele lives in Guildford with her husband and son.

Madhvi Ramani grew up in London, where she studied literature and creative writing at university. She likes dark chocolate, blueberries and second-hand bookshops. She now lives in Berlin, where she spends her time drinking coffee, making stuff up and speaking terrible German. She's currently working on her first novel for teenagers.

Dyan Sheldon is the author of many books for young people, including *Confessions of a Teenage Drama Queen*; *One or Two Things I Learned about Love*; *The Crazy Things Girls Do for Love*; *Tall, Thin and Blonde*; and *My Worst Best Friend*. Dyan was born in Brooklyn and now lives in London.

$\mathcal{S}$arah Webb worked as a children's bookseller for many years before becoming a full-time author. Writing is her dream job as she can travel, read books and magazines, watch TV and movies, and interrogate friends and family, all in the name of "research". Sarah is the author of the much-loved Ask Amy Green series. She has also written ten adult novels and many books for younger children. She visits a school every Friday during term time and loves meeting young readers and writers.

Sarah Webb